D0364056

TORCHWOOD

THE UNDERTAKER'S GIFT

Recent titles in the *Torchwood* series from BBC Books:

9.   ALMOST PERFECT
     James Goss

10. INTO THE SILENCE
     Sarah Pinborough

11. BAY OF THE DEAD
     Mark Morris

12. THE HOUSE THAT JACK BUILT
     Guy Adams

13. RISK ASSESSMENT
     James Goss

14. THE UNDERTAKER'S GIFT
     Trevor Baxendale

15. CONSEQUENCES
     James Moran, Joseph Lidster,
     Andrew Cartmel, Sarah Pinborough
     and David Llewellyn

TORCHWOOD
THE UNDERTAKER'S GIFT

Trevor Baxendale

BOOKS

2 4 6 8 10 9 7 5 3 1

Published in 2009 by BBC Books, an imprint of Ebury Publishing
A Random House Group company

© Trevor Baxendale, 2009
Trevor Baxendale has asserted his right to be identified as the author of this
Work in accordance with the Copyright, Design and Patents Act 1988.

Torchwood is a BBC Wales production for BBC One
Executive Producers: Russell T Davies and Julie Gardner

Original series created by Russell T Davies and broadcast on BBC Television.
'Torchwood' and the Torchwood logo are trademarks of the
British Broadcasting Corporation and are used under licence.

The Random House Group Limited Reg. No. 954009.
Addresses for companies within the Random House Group can be found at
www.randomhouse.co.uk

A CIP catalogue record for this book is available from the British Library.

ISBN 978 1 846 07782 1

The Random House Group Limited supports The Forest Stewardship Council
(FSC), the leading international forest certification organisation.
All our titles that are printed on Greenpeace approved FSC certified paper
carry the FSC logo. Our paper procurement policy can be found at
www.rbooks.co.uk/environment

Commissioning Editor: Albert DePetrillo
Series Editor: Steve Tribe
Production Controller: Phil Spencer

Cover design by Lee Binding @ Tea Lady © BBC 2009
Typeset in Albertina and Century Gothic
Printed and bound in Germany by GGP Media GmbH

For Martine, Luke and Konnie

LAST WEEK

ONE

'Why does it always rain at funerals?' asked Gwen.

'It doesn't,' Jack said. 'It just seems that way.'

They were standing under a large, black umbrella. A heavy, persistent downpour ran off it in streams and spattered onto the turf at their feet.

'It's freezing, too,' muttered Ianto. He clutched the umbrella in one gloved hand, his shoulders hunched miserably inside his black Melton overcoat. It was buttoned up to the collar. His face was pinched and white. 'What are we doing here, exactly?'

'Paying our respects.' Jack was wearing his usual RAF greatcoat, the blue-grey wool speckled black with raindrops. He looked thoughtful and pale, as if the grim weather had sucked out his usual good humour and spat it on the ground.

'And who're we paying our respects to?' asked Gwen, zipping her leather jacket up to her throat.

The mourners had gathered by the side of the grave, huddled together under a large bouquet of umbrellas. The curate was holding one over the vicar as he read solemnly from the Bible, his voice thick with mucous. Occasionally he would stop to wipe at his nose with a handkerchief.

'Thomas Greenway,' Jack said. 'Twenty-one last month. Hit by a bus last week. Didn't look when he crossed the road.'

Gwen looked back at the mourners. 'So what's Torchwood's interest in this?'

'I'm a friend of the family.'

The mourners were glaring at Jack with barely concealed hatred.

'Sort of,' Jack added.

The pallbearers lowered the coffin into the grave, and Jack shuddered. The parents of the deceased were crying now, the mother trying hard not to give in to the wracking sobs that were lining up in her chest.

'Ashes to ashes,' intoned the vicar, trying not to raise his voice over the rain. 'Dust to dust…'

'There's a problem, though,' Jack said quietly.

A sudden, loud banging could be heard, like someone knocking urgently on a door. It was coming from the grave. From inside the coffin. People began to step back, startled and confused.

'He ain't dead yet,' Jack said.

The people by the graveside began to moan in distress as the banging continued. They backed away, further and further, leaving only the vicar. He raised his right hand and drew the sign of the cross over the coffin as the knocking increased in ferocity.

'When Tommy was 5 years old,' continued Jack, 'he was infected by a Magelnian Twort. Nasty little parasite that came through the Rift. Stays dormant until the host body's biologic homeostasis fails and the core temperature drops below a certain level.'

The coffin lid was starting to splinter as it was attacked violently from the inside.

'And then what?' asked Gwen, beginning to wish she had brought a gun.

'It starts to mutate the host, a full-on DNA rewrite. It's been happening since the day Tommy died. I tried to warn his folks, but they wouldn't listen. Insisted on a proper burial, not a cremation.'

With a loud crack the coffin lid burst open and a shrouded figure emerged. The linen fell away to reveal something only vaguely humanoid, covered in flesh like black rubber. The only discernible feature was a suppurating red orifice in the centre of its head. The assembled mourners groaned with revulsion as the hole puckered open to reveal a ring of jagged teeth.

'So I'm afraid it's hello and goodbye,' said Jack, drawing his Webley revolver and shooting the thing through the centre of its head. Mutant brain matter sprayed across the grave, and the corpse fell back into the coffin with a heavy thud.

For a moment all that could be heard was the echo of the shot rolling around the cemetery and the harsh, excited cries of the rooks that had flown out of nearby trees in shock.

Then silence.

'Bloody Torchwood,' said the vicar, taking off his glasses to wipe specks of alien goo from the lenses.

Ianto stepped forward, gently offering the deceased's mother a glass of water. He had seemingly conjured the glass out of thin air. It was a skill that only the very best butlers could master, as Jack would often point out. He loved to tease.

'Here,' Ianto urged softly. 'Drink this.'

Stunned into acquiescence, Mrs Greenway sipped the water. 'That *wasn't* Tommy,' she muttered, dazed. 'That *wasn't* my Tommy…'

'Of course it wasn't,' Ianto assured her.

'Wh-what was it?'

'Allow me to explain.' He led her away from the grave towards the rest of the mourners. The water was laced with Retcon. Ianto was highly skilled in the art of proffering reasonable explanations for unreasonable incidents, and he had a box of the little white pills in his coat pocket. There would be quite a few people needing a drink and an explanation right now.

Gwen had been left with the umbrella. She stood with Jack at the graveside and looked down at the crumpled heap in the coffin. 'I don't think I'll ever get used to this,' she said. 'And I suppose that's probably a good thing.'

'It is,' Jack confirmed. 'I've stood by way too many gravesides. And I've been in a few. It never gets any easier.'

There was a disturbing, faraway look in his eyes. Gwen had seen that look before. She thought of Tosh and Owen, and guessed that Jack had stood over the graves of a great many Torchwood operatives in his time – colleagues and friends, and probably lovers as well. Gwen wondered if he would end up standing by her grave one day. And when she caught the desolate expression in those clear blue eyes as they turned to look at her, she knew he was wondering the same thing.

Gwen struggled for a way to change the subject and found, with relief, that there was something to change it for her. On the far side of the cemetery, ghost-like in the shadow of the slender birches that circled the graveyard, was a thin, dark figure in a long coat. He looked very pale, and he was watching them carefully. Gwen touched Jack's arm. 'Who's that?'

'Trouble,' said Jack, following her gaze.

The spectral figure waited for them to join him beneath the trees. Gwen had mistaken him for another mourner, or perhaps the driver of the hearse – his long, buttoned coat stretched down to his ankles, and he was wearing black gloves. But, close up, Gwen realised that he was not even human. He was preternaturally thin, the skin of his face was as white as chalk, and he was completely hairless. He had grey eyes with vertical pupils and nictitating eyelids. The lips were white, the interior of his mouth blue-black when he spoke.

'Jack!' he hissed by way of greeting. It sounded like an

expletive.

'Do you two know each other?' asked Gwen, slightly irritated by the way the alien was pointedly ignoring her. His goat-like eyes were fixed only on Jack. Nothing unusual there, she supposed.

'Gwen Cooper, meet Harold.'

Gwen blinked. 'Hello, Harold.'

The alien ignored her.

'I don't know his real name,' Jack confessed. 'So I call him Harold. He prefers to remain incognito.'

'I come with a warning,' Harold said, somewhat portentously. He raised a gloved hand to his lips and Gwen was not in the least surprised to see that it held a cigarette. He took a long drag and then blew smoke out through his aquiline nose. 'Your old friends from Hokrala Corp are on the warpath again.'

Jack shrugged. 'I know all about them, Harold. They've been coming here every year since the turn of the century, trying to land a writ on me. Tell me something I don't know.'

'All right,' said Harold, aiming a smoke ring at Gwen.

'Hey,' said Gwen, wafting.

Harold's gaze remained on Jack. 'They're planning more than legal action this time, Jack. Hokrala want you by the balls...'

'Doesn't everyone?'

'... and they're going to squeeze until you scream.'

'I can handle the Hokrala Corp lawyers.'

'Is that a fact? Good for you.' Harold took a long drag on his cigarette. 'But I happen to know that they're planning something a little more fatal than a writ this time. Word is they've hired an assassin.'

Jack laughed. 'An assassin?'

'Yes. They want you out of the way – permanently.'

'They're going to find that a bit difficult,' mused Gwen.

Harold gave a minute shrug. 'Please yourselves. Don't say I didn't warn you.'

'OK.' Jack straightened his face and nodded. 'Thanks for the tip-off. But, really, I think we can handle it.'

Harold sighed theatrically. 'You always were the glib one, Jack – silver of tongue and pert of cheek. But listen to a word of advice from an old *acquaintance*.' He pronounced the word 'acquaintance' in a way that quite clearly differentiated it from 'friend'.

Jack's eyes narrowed fractionally. He could sense trouble. 'What is it?'

'I don't know the full details, but I do know that the Hokrala people are worried – very worried – that things are about to go somewhat awry for Earth in the twenty-first century.'

'Tell them not to worry. We've got it covered.'

'Hmm. Torchwood.' Harold looked as if he had just licked the bottom of his shoe. 'Well, that could just be the problem.'

'Meaning what, exactly?' Gwen asked.

Harold glanced at her and sniffed, as if he was reluctant to even speak to her. 'They don't think Torchwood can handle it.'

'Handle what?'

'The twenty-first century.'

'Hokrala's beef is with me,' said Jack, bristling. 'Hell, they can send their assassin if they want. Good luck to him.'

Harold took a drag on his cigarette and blew a smoke ring at Gwen. 'Have it your own way, dear boy. But don't say I didn't warn you.'

And with that Harold flicked away the cigarette with a sharp, reptilian movement of his fingers. Gwen watched it land in a flowerbed, and when she looked back Harold had disappeared. Completely.

'Hey!' she said.

'Teleport,' Jack said, checking the readings on his wrist-strap. He let out a hiss of impatience. 'Show-off.'

LAST NIGHT

TWO

Rachel 'Ray' Banks hurried through the darkened streets of Cardiff. According to her watch it was nearly 4 a.m. There was absolutely no one else about, and the emptiness was starting to creep her out. She stopped at a deserted crossroads. The street lamps were on, the orange sodium glare reflecting on the ice-wet tarmac like night-time mirages. There was no one about. Not a soul. It was as if Ray had the entire city to herself.

It was seriously starting to feel a bit freaky now.

Maybe she should have taken Gillian's advice and stayed on at the party. At least Ray would have had a place to crash for the night, even if it had meant fending off the more amorous – or drunk – partygoers. And it wasn't a great sign when even Gillian's advice sounded good.

'Don't tell me you're going *already*?' She recalled Gillian's aghast expression quite clearly. Ray had explained – as patiently as she could when yelling over Lily Allen's 'Not Fair' at full blast – that she had a lecture first thing in the morning and really ought to be leaving.

'A *lecture*?' Gillian appeared not to understand the word. And she was actually frowning. 'First thing?'

'Yes,' Ray had said. 'Heath Park at 10.30. I really want to go.'

Gillian now looked shocked. 'But you can't go *now*,' she screamed. Ray could barely hear her. 'It's just getting good. And besides, you don't want to be walking home alone. That's *not* good.'

But Ray had always been strong-willed – some would have said stubborn – and there was nothing more guaranteed to make her do something than somebody telling her *not* to do it. Her parents had found that out at an early age – which, ultimately, was a good part of the reason why Ray had ended up studying Ecology at Cardiff University rather than working in her mother's flower shop in Bristol.

She checked her watch again: 4.10 a.m. The streets were still empty, and she stopped to listen carefully. A bus or a taxi would be good right now. In the distance she thought she heard a car engine accelerating away; it sounded like the last person on Earth just leaving.

Alone, cold, lost, Ray walked on. She didn't even know what direction she should go in. She thought she knew Cardiff quite well, but it all looked different at four in the morning and she guessed she was probably slightly drunk.

How else could she explain why she was so lost? The party had been in a house owned by another student's parents who were away on holiday. There had been forty or fifty people in that house, with loads of booze, music, sex (probably) and the chance to emerge dazed and tired in the early hours of the morning. And then get hopelessly lost.

The house was somewhere around Cyncoed, she was pretty certain of that. Or was it Llanedeyrn? Her halls of residence were just off Colum Road but that might as well have been Glasgow from here.

Ray cursed herself for not leaving with Wynnie when she'd had the chance. Wynnie had left at half one. A sensible time. Wynnie would be home by now, probably asleep in a nice warm bed, an empty cup of cocoa on the floor.

Ray crossed a road called Carner Lane and cut through between a small row of semis to another avenue. If she followed the slope of the road down, she thought she would at least be heading back into the city centre. She could pick up a taxi on the way if necessary.

Twenty minutes later she was still lost, had still not seen or heard any sign of another living thing and was seriously starting to worry. She hurried past a small patch of scrubby grass surrounded by old, bent railings covered in rust.

Where was everyone? Just because it was 4.30-ish in the morning, and freezing cold, didn't mean that everyone was tucked up in bed like Wynnie, surely? What about the shift workers? Police? Anyone?

Ray turned a corner at random, her trainers scuffing the tarmac with short, panicky steps. She was pretty scared now. She thought about phoning Gillian but, quite apart from the fact that Ray didn't want to endure a drunken 'I told you so' conversation, Gillian was famously useless in a crisis. Ray felt she had to speak to *someone*, though, so she took out her mobile and dialled Wynnie instead.

The phone rang a few times and then switched to voicemail: 'Wynnie. Call you back. Bye.'

Ray snapped the phone shut with a curse and cut across a square surrounded by a line of old, bare trees. There was a building up ahead – she couldn't see it very clearly in the dark, but perhaps there would be a bus stop or something on the far side.

She cut quickly through the trees and then stopped in her tracks.

She had stumbled across some kind of derelict church – it was practically in ruins, surrounded by some trees and scrubby grass and cracked pavements.

And there were people here.

A dozen or so, standing silently in the gloom. They were wearing long coats and top hats. Some held walking sticks or canes. Something about the whole scene made Ray's insides turn cold. Perhaps it was the clothes, which, on closer inspection, looked old and stained, with frayed hems and ragged sleeves. Their heads appeared to be wrapped in dark scarves and they were wearing sunglasses, which was odd at 4.30 in the morning. The lenses of the nearest man flashed in the streetlights as he turned to look at Ray.

She wanted to turn and run, she really did, but she just couldn't move. Something made her stand and stare back at him.

His face was completely hidden by the filthy bandages wound all around his head. His eyes were concealed behind the glasses, but he seemed to be looking straight at her, almost through her. Ray felt her skin crawling. Then the man raised his arm – showing his hand to be encased in threadbare gloves mottled with greasy stains – and this seemed to be a signal for the others to move.

Because, most oddly, the men were all standing in two distinct lines, as if they were in some kind of a procession. The leading men, the ones holding the long, spear-tipped canes, began to march forward at a slow, steady pace.

And at that moment Ray saw the whole thing for what it was, in a moment of chilling clarity.

It was a funeral cortège. Because the final six men were carrying a long, glass-walled casket as if they were pallbearers.

And as it drew alongside, Ray could see the contents of the casket, illuminated by the harsh yellow street light above.

She stared, long and hard, unable to look away. Her heart was pounding in her chest and the contents of her stomach churned.

Then she turned and threw up on the pavement.

LAST CHANCE

THREE

His mouth was full of soil.

He'd been screaming, and the wet earth had gone straight in. He choked and tried to get up, but the weight of the dirt was too much. More soil poured down, stones and twigs bouncing off his skull and worms twisting around his face and neck.

He had to get out. He was lying in a grave for Christ's sake, and he was being *buried alive*. He had to get out.

But the soil kept coming, and eventually he couldn't see anything. The weight was incredible – cold, wet, heavy earth, pressing down on his face and chest like a giant heel grinding him deeper into the hole.

There was grit in his eyes and ears and he couldn't even *move* now, let alone breathe. The dirt closed over his head, and for a while all he could hear was the muffled thump of each shovelful landing on top of him and the thick rush of blood in his head. He was going to die.

Again.

How long would it take this time? How long would it take to die – and how long would it take to *live*?

'Jack?'

He lurched awake with a sudden, vast gulp of air. It was dark, but there was nothing on top of him other than a bed sheet.

'Bad dream?' Gwen Cooper asked. She was standing at the end of his bed, watching him, smiling.

'Yeah. I get a lot of those now.'

'It's only to be expected,' Gwen told him. She sat down on the bed next to him, naked. 'After all you've been through.'

Jack smiled and reached out to her, stroking the bare flesh of her arm. It was cool and creamy in the darkness. Her hair hung like a thick black curtain over her shoulders, and her eyes glittered. Jack's gaze travelled down her face and neck, examining the curves, looking for any imperfections and finding none.

'You are wonderful,' he told her truthfully.

'I know,' she whispered, leaning in to take his kiss. Jack reached up, cupping the back of her head in his hand and pressing his lips onto hers. She tasted of clear mountain stream water, cold and refreshing and full of life. Jack pulled her down onto the bed, turning her over so that he could look down into her eyes.

Gwen's eyes were incredible; huge, dark pools that could take you down, deeper than Time. She gazed up at him, languid and adoring. He kissed her again, climbing on top of her.

'Where is everyone?' he asked, without quite knowing why. A twinge of guilt?

'They're dead, Jack,' she replied. 'They're all dead.'

Jack frowned. He wanted to kiss her again, but something was niggling at the back of his mind. Something wasn't right.

'Do you forgive me, Jack?' Gwen asked.

'Forgive you?' He gave an uneasy laugh. 'What for?'

'Killing them all, of course. You can be so silly at times, can't you, Jack?'

'What are you talking about?'

'I had to make the choice. Remember? I had to kill one person to save everyone else. That was the choice you gave me.'

'Choice?'

She was smiling at him in the darkness but she was hurting him as well. Her fingernails were digging into the flesh of his shoulders like claws, and now he realised that the warm, tickling sensation on the skin of his back was not the gentle caress of her fingertips, but the blood running out of the scratches she had made.

'Gwen!' he gasped, like a lover in climax. 'Let go!'

'I'll never let you go, Jack,' she told him, and the claws sunk deeper into his flesh until he could feel them scraping on the bones of his shoulders. He tried to push himself off her, but she was hanging on with a fierce, agonising grip. Her legs folded around his waist and suddenly he felt as if she was going to crush him.

'Let me go!'

'*Never.*'

She was still smiling, her face completely relaxed and showing no sign of strain. And yet Jack was pulling away from her with all his strength. The muscles were hardening under his skin, sinews straining, but it had no effect. He might have been a child in her arms. He started to cry, tears falling onto her face. She laughed and opened her mouth to catch them.

'Please!' Jack cried. 'Please stop!'

'I killed them all, Jack,' she repeated. 'Every last human being on the planet. It's just us now – you and me. And I'll never let you go.'

'The hell you won't!' Jack roared. He closed his hands around her neck and squeezed, pushing his thumbs deep into the soft part of her throat to close off the windpipe. He gritted his teeth and bore down on her, determined to kill.

But she just smiled at him as if she couldn't feel pain and didn't need to breathe.

And then something occurred to him, a tiny detail that was as obvious now as the pain from his lacerated back: she had no pulse. He had his fingers clamped around her neck and he could not feel a pulse. She was already dead. But she hadn't stopped smiling.

When she opened her mouth, he saw that it was full of earth, black and crumbling and twisting with moist, pink life. With a final, choking cry Jack tore himself free, hurling himself off her, tangled up in the sweat-cold sheets.

'Bad dream?' asked Ianto politely.

Jack sat up abruptly, blinking in the sudden bright light. He was panting hard and he could feel the perspiration on his neck and chest. The sheets were twisted around him but he was alone in the bed.

Ianto stood at the base of the bed, suited and booted. He looked ready for business. 'I don't dream,' said Jack eventually. It had taken a while to get his breath back. 'I don't even sleep. Not properly. You know that.'

Ianto gently placed the fresh mug of coffee on the bedside table. 'What are you doing in bed, then? Alone, I mean?'

Jack watched Ianto warily for a few seconds before replying. 'I don't know. Thinking. Drifting. Dreaming, I suppose.'

'Sometimes I think you could do with some proper sleep.'

'I doubt it.' Jack picked up the coffee and sipped it, considering. 'It was a nightmare.' He sounded confused, as if a nightmare was the very last thing he expected. 'I was being buried alive. No surprise there, I guess. But this was… different…' He didn't want to go into any detail about Gwen now. That was one fantasy that had to be kept under lock and key.

'Perhaps it was the pizza last night. Too much cheese before bedtime.'

Jack shook his head, not in the mood for jokes. 'How's Gwen?'

'Fine – as far as I know. Rhys has gone to a hauliers' convention or something in Gloucester. She misses him but otherwise she's OK. Why? Shouldn't she be?'

'I don't know.'

26

Ianto started to lay Jack's clothes out. 'Gwen told me about the alien at Tommy Greenway's funeral last week. I believe we can expect another visit from our friends at Hokrala.'

'Yeah.' Jack climbed out of bed. He was naked, and Ianto suddenly felt absurdly overdressed in his three-piece pinstripe and silk tie. But Jack didn't seem to notice. 'That's not what's bothering me,' he said.

'Then what is?'

Jack headed for the shower. 'When you've lived in one place for long enough you get a feeling for it. You can tell when something's wrong.'

He ran the water and stepped behind the frosted glass. Steam filled the cubicle as the water heated up and Jack became a pink blur.

'And something is wrong, then?' Ianto asked.

'You said it. There's so much coming through the Rift at the moment – it doesn't feel right.'

'It *has* been unusually active recently,' Ianto agreed, taking a notebook out of his pocket and flipping it open. 'We've been rushed off our feet since Jackson Leaves and the xXltttxtolxtol. And of course, um, Agnes…'

Jack flinched, but Ianto carried on regardless.

'Then there was the Greenway funeral, and the Fairwater Death Sticks. There's been a Grolon rat infestation in Butetown. Couple of Blowfish low-lifes loose in Splott. Our electrical friend in Cell One… The list goes on. In fact, we've never been so busy.'

'I know, I know,' Jack said, splashing. The water had flattened his hair over his face. 'But it's not that. There's something else.'

Ianto watched the islands of soap lather shift like continents over the vague shape of Jack's chest before being rinsed away.

'I don't know what it is,' Jack continued, 'but I can *feel* it. Something bad is coming our way, Ianto.'

Ianto watched for another full minute as Jack let the hot water stream down his shoulders and back before asking, 'Care for some company in there?'

Jack's blue eyes flicked open, the lashes thick and wet. 'No,' he said. 'Not right now.'

FOUR

Ray was sitting in Wynnie's flat, hugging a cushion.

'You look totally wrecked,' observed Wynnie. He placed a mug of tea on the low table in front of her.

Ray didn't even look up. Her fingers were white where they dug into the old velveteen cushion.

Wynnie cleared a space on the coffee table, pushing aside a pile of music magazines, research papers and empty cans of Red Bull so he could sit down. Then he faced Ray and stared at her until she did look up.

'Never thought I'd see the day when you were lost for words,' he told her. 'Must've been a hell of a party.'

'Hell of a party,' she repeated dully. 'Good one.'

'Here,' Wynnie pushed the tea towards her. 'Drink. It's got sugar in it. Looks like you could do with it.'

'What do you mean?'

'You're in shock. That much is obvious. Drink the tea and then tell me what happened. From the beginning. From when you left the party.'

He gently removed the cushion and gave her the mug of tea.

'I think I saw a little bit of hell last night,' she said.

'Care to expand on that?'

So she told him. Everything.

When she'd finished, pale and trembling, she sipped the tea. Wynnie sat back and stuck out his bottom lip. On anyone else it would look like a sulk. On Wynnie, it meant he was thinking. Behind the lip rings, tongue piercing, eyebrow studs and blond dreadlocks, there was a first-class brain breezing through the final year of a postgraduate Chemistry course. Some people said Wynnie was only doing the Ph.D. in his spare time, when he wasn't playing bass guitar in his band or drawing comics for the student rag.

'So,' Ray said at last. 'Do you think I'm going bonkers, then? Cos I do.'

'You're sure no one slipped you anything at the party?'

'Absolutely sure.'

'No one tampered with your drinks?'

'No way.'

'You didn't drop any tabs? Not even E?'

'Nothing. I was a tiny bit pissed but that's all. Not so I couldn't walk home on my own. Just a bit… you know…'

'And this thing in the casket…'

Ray's eyes snapped shut. 'I don't want to talk about it. Not any more. I don't even want to *think* about it.'

'OK. Fine. Here's what we'll do. We'll go back to the place you saw these guys, now, in broad daylight. Check it out, see if there's anything there.'

Ray opened an eye, glared suspiciously at him. 'What, like evidence you mean?'

'I dunno. Anything. You never know.'

'There won't be anything. It all just disappeared. Like a… like a…'

'Dream?'

'Like a nightmare.'

FIVE

The SUV cruised along Penarth Road with Jack at the wheel. He seemed distracted, braking late and accelerating with undue aggression. The engine growled impatiently as the big black chassis muscled its way through the morning traffic.

In the passenger seat, Gwen was reloading a customised automatic. It was a Glock 19, a compact, lightweight nylon-based polymer-frame pistol Ianto had given her to field-test. She snapped a full magazine into the butt – fifteen rounds of tungsten-core 9mm parabellum – and pulled back the slide to load the first cartridge into the firing chamber.

'So, these Hokrala people. We met them last year, didn't we?' she asked.

'The last time we saw them was just after the Strepto hag business,' Ianto confirmed from the rear seat. He was examining the computer displays mounted into the backs of the front seats. 'We get a visit almost every year. They're lawyers, apparently. From the future.'

'Hokrala Corp's a big-shot law firm from the forty-ninth century,' said Jack. 'They have access to warp-shunt technology and they've been trying to land a writ on Torchwood for years.'

'A writ?' Gwen frowned. 'What, you mean they're trying to sue us? What for?'

'Screwing up.'

'Come again?'

'They want to sue us for mishandling the twenty-first century,' Jack explained, giving the steering wheel a sudden yank and sending the SUV into a tight right hander. The big tyres snarled across the tarmac.

'When it all changes,' Ianto added helpfully.

'But Torchwood's been going for *ages* – I mean, since Queen Victoria's time,' argued Gwen.

'Yeah,' nodded Jack. 'But aliens have been coming to Earth since the dawn of time. The Silurians, the Neolithics, Egyptians, Greeks, Aztecs, Incas, even the Spanish Inquisition – they've all claimed first contact at some point.'

'So why are we the lucky ones then? And who the hell were the Silurians?' Gwen grabbed an armrest as the SUV swerved through the traffic. 'Why are these Hokrala people so interested in Torchwood?'

'Could be because of the Rift,' Ianto said. 'Maybe it gives them access to the twenty-first century.'

'Makes sense, I suppose.'

'And then there's me,' Jack said.

'You?'

'Hokrala and I go back a long way. Or is that forward? It's hard to say – but either way, it's personal. They just don't like me.'

'Why? What've you done?'

'Annoyed them, big time,' Jack said. 'You'll see. It didn't surprise me when Harold said they were gonna have me assassinated. They've been itching to do that for years.'

'Who is this Harold person, exactly?' Ianto asked.

Jack grinned. 'He's a rogue. A hustler.'

'So we're taking the word of a *conman*?' Ianto looked pained. 'That doesn't exactly fill me with confidence.'

'Hey,' Jack said. 'Not all conmen are bad people. I used to be a bit of a grifter myself.'

'Grifter?'

'Haven't you ever watched *Hustle?*'

'No,' Ianto replied carefully.

Gwen tapped the GPS. 'OK, boys. We're nearly there. Ianto?'

'Rift activity symptomatic of temporal incursion in the Leckwith area,' Ianto reported, checking the monitors again. 'It's the Hokrala chronon-energy signature all right. They're coming through. Sending the exact coordinates to the GPS now…'

The dashboard computers chirruped and the satnav screen planned a route. Jack tooled the SUV down a side street and into a car park. They got out, but there didn't seem to be anything out of the ordinary. Parked cars, Pay-and-Display machines, litter. The faint smell of engine oil and petrol.

Jack's shoulders flexed under his greatcoat. 'Feel that?'

Gwen and Ianto looked at him and shook their heads.

'Static electricity. It's in the air. It's a warp shunt. They're comin'.'

Ianto was checking his PDA scanner. 'Not picking up anything here – oh. Wait.' His faced creased into a sudden frown. 'Gosh, the reading's gone off the scale.'

'Can't see anything,' Gwen said, turning slowly in a circle. She pulled a strand of hair off her face and shuddered. There was something. A kind of tang in the air, like just before a storm.

Suddenly all the parked cars sounded their horns at once. There was no one inside the cars; the horns blew by themselves, a long, screeching note of alarm. The headlights lit up and indicators flashed madly, as if all the cars were signalling urgently to them to get out of the way.

'Just our luck,' said Ianto, swallowing nervously. 'A Herbie convention.'

And then, with sudden, shocking force, about twenty cars were completely flattened as if a giant, invisible hand had smacked them all flat like matchboxes. The vehicles at the epicentre were squashed into tin foil and strips of rubber as an immense pressure wave of cold, oily air knocked Jack, Ianto and Gwen off their feet. Cars on the perimeter were half-crushed – their bonnets slapped down into the concrete, rear ends bouncing up into the air with a deafening clatter.

The damage described a perfect hemisphere, as if the underside of a super-dense, invisible ball had landed right in the middle of the car park. At the very centre of the sphere were three men in silvery-grey suits. The central, taller figure was flanked by two brutish, ape-like thugs. They were carrying huge automatic weapons in long, powerful arms. They walked calmly down from six metres in the air until they were standing directly in front of the Torchwood operatives.

Jack was helping Gwen to her feet. She always hated it when he did that, but there was a strong whiff of the old-fashioned about Jack that said more about him than the Second World War RAF look.

Ianto was trying to scan with the PDA but the equipment now seemed to be faulty.

The leader of the dark men stepped slowly forward, peeling off a pair of thin black gloves from white hands. He looked human – but only just. His skin was so pale that it was almost transparent. Blue veins and pink muscle could be seen moving under his pallid flesh. His eyes were hidden behind mirrored sunglasses, but his attention was clearly focused on Jack.

'Harkness.'

Jack straightened up. 'That's *Captain* Harkness to you.'

'You know why we're here. Pursuant to Section 4 Paragraph 25 of the Future Time Edict dated E5150 pro-Hok Gibbon slash Kulkana, we are suing you – personally – for mishandling the twenty-first century.'

'It's barely begun.'

The alien shrugged, unmoved. 'Face it, Harkness. You've

blown it already. Our records show a catalogue of failures leading right up to this moment – the time of your greatest fiasco.' He reached inside his coat and produced a slim envelope, which he proffered towards Jack.

'Surely we can appeal?' asked Ianto, stepping forward to take the envelope.

The lawyer shook his head. 'There is no appeal process.'

'Sure there is,' said Jack, drawing his Webley and aiming it at the lawyer's forehead. Gwen and Ianto produced their own automatics on cue, aiming at the two henchmen.

The lawyer waved his hand dismissively and Jack's pistol glowed red hot, forcing him to release it. 'Ow!'

'What a pathetic piece of ironmongery,' said the lawyer, prodding the gun with the toe of his boot. 'A relic even in this time period. A symbol of your failed attempt to integrate with this era, Harkness.'

Gwen and Ianto were quietly holstering their own weapons. 'You wouldn't be so tough if it wasn't for those two gorillas,' muttered Ianto.

'Yeah,' agreed Gwen. 'And those big guns – they've got to be compensating for something. Am I right, boys?'

The apes leered at her.

'We come only lightly armed,' the leader informed her. 'If we meant you any physical harm, we would simply sink this island.'

It took Gwen a moment or two to realise what he meant. And then the scale of the threat almost overwhelmed her.

'It's been done before,' shrugged the lawyer, noting her look of incredulity.

'Let's leave Atlantis out of this,' said Jack. 'I think we're all agreed it wasn't exactly the Time Agency's greatest success.'

'You should know,' retorted the lawyer archly.

'Wait a minute,' said Gwen. 'If we can't appeal against this writ thing then surely we can negotiate?'

'Negotiate?' repeated the lawyer. 'Don't understand the word.'

Ianto said, 'It means…'

He realised that the apes were laughing at him and their leader was smiling indulgently.

'Hold it,' said Jack. 'OK, so we may not be on top of absolutely everything. But we've done some pretty good stuff. We saw off Abaddon for a start. Your records show that?'

The lawyer rolled his eyes impatiently. 'You were lucky.'

'What about the alien sleepers, then? Cell 114?' asked Gwen. 'They were going to nuke the whole of South Wales. And what about the Pharm?'

'And don't forget that CERN business,' added Ianto. 'Did you hear about that?'

'Minor successes owing more to luck than judgement,' responded the lawyer tartly. 'What about the things left undone? There is a spatial rupture on the seabed two miles off the coast that continues to spew proto-organic waste into the ocean. It's an environmental disaster happening while you stand here and you've done absolutely nothing to stop it.'

Gwen pulled a disgusted face. 'Oh, don't start playing the green card. That's so cheap.'

'You've got your time lines crossed, anyway,' said Jack. 'It's already sorted. I checked that out a year ago. There's a fissure at the bottom of the bay regurgitating calcified amino-acids from the Palaeocene era. We ran a complete chemical composition analysis on it last year – the complex nutrients and bio-chemicals contained in the stuff breaks down industrial oil and pollutants. So it's actually improving the quality of the seawater. By our calculations, in another hundred years or so the South Wales coastline will have the purest saltwater anywhere on the planet since before the Industrial Revolution.'

The lawyer snorted. 'Your time's up, Harkness. The twenty-first century is when it all *ends*.'

'Wait a sec. What do you mean by that, exactly?'

'Don't you know?'

Jack raised an eyebrow. 'Give me a clue.'

The lawyer seemed highly amused. 'Haven't you heard of the Undertaker's Gift?'

Both Gwen and Ianto saw the minute change that came over Jack then: not a flinch, as such, but an imperceptible stiffening of the shoulders. It is doubtful whether anyone else would have noticed it. And then, after the barest pause, Jack's eyes narrowed. 'Is this some kind of test?'

'Test?' The lawyer looked appalled. 'The Undertaker's Gift isn't a *test*, Harkness. It's far too serious for that. But let's say that if it *were* a test, then you've already failed it. And the consequences will be disastrous. Catastrophic, in fact.'

'Meaning what, exactly?' Gwen demanded. She could see that, for whatever reason, Jack had been momentarily thrown by the merest mention of this Undertaker's Gift. She guessed that he knew exactly what it meant, but she had no idea. And she wanted to know. Because anything that could throw Jack Harkness off his stride had to be something bad. She looked squarely at the lawyer and repeated her question: 'I said what does it mean? What is the Undertaker's Gift?'

The lawyer touched a finger to his lips. 'A world of suffering.'

And with that, the legal team disappeared in a fizz of energy, and several squashed cars gave a pathetic rattle.

'They've gone,' said Ianto, a little awed.

'People keep doing that to me these days,' complained Jack.

Ianto was looking at the envelope in his hand. 'And they served us with a writ.'

'Yeah.' A hard, slightly anxious look had clouded Jack's sky-blue eyes. 'I would have preferred an assassin.'

SIX

And the nightmares keep on coming!

It's getting to be a real bugger cos I'm not even asleep.

It's the same thing all the time:

I'm on my way to a home I can't find and don't know where it is. I'm lost and cold. And then I come across a funeral. For tramps. It's like a procession, creepy and almost Victorian, but these guys are wearing scuzzy old clothes and rags and I can't see their faces at all. This is way weird, but the pallbearers are wearing masks. Well, not masks but sort of bandages. Like the Invisible Man.

They look at me, right, even though I can't see their eyes cos their faces are just blank and some of them are wearing stupid little sunglasses. But then they just kind of ignore me and the procession goes on. And the casket draws up level with me and it's made of glass or something cos I can see right inside it.

By now I'm completely freaked out. I'm sweating just typing it up now. I'm sweating when I wake up and I'm shivering too and my heart's racing like mad.

But I never wake up in time.

I never wake up before I see what's inside the casket.

And that's the thing that stays with me even when I'm awake, like *it's been burned into my brain or something. It's like the image has been branded onto my optic nerves. OK, so that's a bit on the melodramatic side, but it's so getting on my tits now. Like it won't give up till I'm completely mad.*

Wynnie thinks I should see someone – a psychologist probably. He hasn't said it out loud but I know that's what he's thinking. Soft sod means well but he's a bloke at the end of the day and what does he know? He says there's a special force called Torchwood that looks into all this kind of crap. A bit like the X-Files I suppose but in Cardiff. Yeah! Right!

I'm supposed to be going to a lecture this morning but somehow 'Landfill Waste and Ecology' just doesn't seem so important or interesting right now. I need to get my head around last night.

So maybe you're reading this and think I'm nuts – or worse, just an attention-seeking drama queen. But those who actually know me won't think either.

Cheerio till next time.

Ray.

She hit Enter, and the blog entry uploaded. She didn't feel any better for it, but at least getting it out there in the public domain felt like she had responded in some way. The thought of keeping it all to herself – or even just Wynnie – was pretty much unbearable.

'You didn't mention that stuff about Torchwood, did you?' Wynnie asked from his position on the sofa. He had his acoustic guitar on his knee, and he was plucking out the chords for 'Unforgiven' by Metallica.

'Um,' said Ray. 'You did say it was just a rumour. Internet scuttlebutt.'

'And I also said don't mention it in your blog.'

'No you didn't.'

'Well I *should* have told you not to mention it in your blog.' His shoulders slumped a little. 'Never mind. It's all rubbish anyway, probably.'

'*Probably?*'

Wynnie shrugged. 'It's something Nina mentioned to me.'

'Who?'

'You know, Nina Rogers – Jessica Montague's best mate. She was doing a load of research into this Torchwood thing on the net.'

'Big deal.'

'Yeah. But I reckon if anything like Torchwood really *did* exist then they'd have got us by now.'

'What do you mean, "got us"?'

'You know. Taken us away. Made us disappear.' A little light went on inside Wynnie's head as an idea struck him, and he put his guitar down, warming to this new subject. 'Or else they'd have just made us forget. Wiped our memories – like in *Men In Black*.'

'But I don't know anything about Torchwood, so there's nothing for me to forget.' She smiled. Then frowned. 'Unless they've already got to me, of course.'

'Good point. Maybe I should mention that to Nina.' He stood up. 'How are you feeling now, anyway?'

Ray sighed, thinking. 'Better, I think. I keep getting these flashbacks though. The things I saw. I can't seem to forget them.'

'It'll take time. Bound to. The images will fade, eventually. I'm sure of it.'

Ray wasn't convinced. She rubbed at the goose bumps on her arms.

'I dunno. This doesn't feel like something I'll ever forget. It's right there in my head, every minute. It's not like a memory... It's more like a mental link or something. A direct, permanent connection to that moment in time and space.'

Wynnie raised his eyebrows. 'OK, now you're sounding weird even by my standards. Drink the tea and let's go.'

Ray nodded, but in her mind's eye she kept seeing the

pallbearers, their bandaged faces turning to look at her. The glass casket.

The thing inside.

Nothing was going to make it go away.

SEVEN

Gwen was driving the SUV back to the Hub. 'This Undertaker's Gift… ' She shot a fast, questioning look at Jack in the passenger seat. 'You know what it is, don't you?'

Jack shrugged. 'I'm not sure. If it's what I think it is, then we're in trouble.'

'Well, I sort of guessed it wouldn't be good news.'

Jack's eyes were cloudy again. 'It's been a Torchwood rumour for as long as I can remember. The people who ran Torchwood in the old days – and I mean the *old* days – used to talk about it in whispers. It was one of those things we were always supposed to be on the lookout for, according to Gerald Kneale. Thankfully, it never came my way.'

'Until now,' Gwen said.

'Maybe.' Jack pulled a face. 'The Undertaker's Gift is almost mythical – I was never convinced it really existed. It was the bogeyman. A threat that was never substantiated.'

'Hokrala seemed very sure about it.'

'Well, they would. It's their job to be very sure about everything. That's their problem – no creativity, no room for inspired guesswork. Hopeless gamblers.'

'What is the Undertaker's Gift, then?' asked Ianto. 'According to legend?'

'It was generally considered to be some kind of planetary threat – the end of the world. The big bad daddy of all atomic bombs – at least that's what we used to think, back in the fifties, until we realised it was more than that. A whole lot more.'

Jack fell silent for a moment and Gwen glanced across at him. He was looking unusually drawn; although he was keeping his tone light, she guessed that he was trying to disguise how rattled he was.

'I think it's some kind of temporal fusion device,' he said. 'Literally, a Time Bomb. I've got no proof of that, by the way. It's just a theory. But it's just about the only thing that could turn this planet inside out – if it was strategically detonated near the Rift, it would split the local time-space continuum wide open. Earth would be wiped out in a temporal spasm that would leave the entire solar system irradiated with fast-decay chronon fallout. Not good.'

'But who would want to do a thing like that?' Gwen wondered.

'It ain't a friendly universe,' Jack said. 'There's folks out there who are queuin' up to have a pop at planet Earth.'

'And why's it called the Undertaker's Gift?' asked Ianto.

'I've no idea. This is the whole problem: not enough hard information, too much speculation. Fear of the unknown does the rest.'

'What can we do?' Gwen asked, trying to think practically. 'Maybe if we could find it…'

'It's never been found,' Jack reminded her. 'It's never even been proven to exist.'

'Could it be a bluff?' Ianto asked.

'Can we take that risk?' Gwen replied.

Ianto held up the Hokrala envelope. 'Looks like the writ will have to take a back seat.'

'Let's not ignore it,' Jack said. 'It could tell us something. Run it through the translator when you get back to the Hub, see what they've got on us. Knowing Hokrala Corp, it'll be about five hundred miles of red tape but there might be something in there that can point us in the right direction. It's not much, but it's all we've got to go on.'

'And to think I was hoping for a couple of days off,' Gwen said ruefully. She took a deep breath. 'Rhys is staying over in Gloucester and I was hoping to join him there if I had the chance…'

Jack shook his head. 'I can't afford to let you go just now. We need to get on top of this Undertaker's Gift thing as well as everything else, just in case. Get on to it, Gwen – use those cop instincts. Run some scans for anything that might be a temporal fusion device – if it's really here it's bound to be in the vicinity of the Rift.'

'Lucky old Cardiff.'

'And you need to keep checking on our guest in Cell One. See if you can't get him to talk any – he's come through the Rift only recently, so he might know something.'

Gwen thought about the alien life form that had been sitting in the Hub's premier holding cell for the last week. 'He hasn't said a word so far,' she argued. 'He hasn't even *moved*. What makes you think I'll have any luck?'

'Use your feminine wiles on him.'

Gwen never really knew if Jack was winding her up when he spoke like this. He came from the far future but sometimes he sounded so old-fashioned. 'Jack,' she said with as much patience as she could muster, 'we are talking about a big blob of electric jelly. What good are feminine wiles?'

'I've asked the same question a thousand times,' smiled Jack. He pointed out of the windscreen. 'You can drop me off here.'

'Here?' Puzzled, Gwen pulled the SUV over by a row of derelict shops. The dark mouth of an alleyway yawned at them.

'Not a very nice area,' commented Ianto.

'There are no nice areas in our line of work,' said Jack darkly. He got out and shut the door behind him.

'What are you going to do?'

'I'm going fishing. See what I can find. Catch you guys later.'

And with that he was gone, striding into the shadows of the alleyway with a flare of his greatcoat.

'I hate it when he does that,' muttered Gwen. 'He so likes to be the centre of attention.'

Ianto frowned. 'He has been acting a little strange lately. Distracted. Mysterious.'

'You got that too?'

'Some might even say grumpy.'

'Some might say Bashful, Sleepy and Sneezy. But I say *worried*.' Gwen's eyes narrowed. 'Something's on Captain Jack's mind, and I wish I knew what it was.'

EIGHT

The cat arched its back, ears flattened, fangs bared. It stood rigid, hackles raised. Its tail had expanded to a fantastic size and in the cat's own mind it looked huge, ferocious, terrifying. Nothing would dare to attack it now.

Three seconds later it was dead, seized by the throat and shaken so hard its neck snapped like a twig. The limp body was then hurled contemptuously against a wall and ignored.

'No fun!' squawked a voice. 'No fun! Too quick!'

A heavy, squat creature with dull, warty skin scuttled over to the corpse and devoured it in a single wet gulp.

Another joined it, bounding along on outsized, disjointed legs. Gimlet eyes stared in the shadows, nostrils twitching at the sweet scent of fresh blood. Both creatures resembled enormous frogs. For a moment they sat and stared at each other, utterly immobile.

'Make 'em fight!' snarled the voice. 'Make 'em fight!'

The nearest toad received a hefty kick and it jumped in the general direction of its mate, whose mouth gaped open in a reflexive hiss, showing rows of shark-like teeth still smeared with blood and cat fur.

'No good, man!' complained the voice. 'Fight! Fight, you little runts!'

There were two of them, wearing hoodies and dark, waterproof coats with baggy tracksuit pants and new trainers. Here, at the bottom of the alleyway, it was impossible to see their faces.

'Hi, boys,' said Jack Harkness.

The hoodies swung around. The toads growled at their feet.

'Now that's what I call antisocial behaviour,' Jack said. 'Don't you guys know that pitbullfrogs are illegal in this time zone?'

There was a glint of streetlight on metal as one of the thugs produced a knife.

Jack raised the Webley. 'Put the blade down, kid, I'm not here to play games.'

But the thug took a step forward, dropping into a fighting crouch, knife extended. As the owner moved out of the shadows his face became visible beneath the hood of his jacket: cold, angry eyes glared out from glistening, crimson flesh and a multitude of spines quivered around an ugly, puckered mouth.

'Human scum!' it hissed.

Jack sighed. 'Great. Just what the world needs – Blowfish hoodies.'

'Stick 'im, Kerko!' ordered the second hoodie, and the kid with the knife lunged obediently. Jack stepped inside the thrusting blade, cracked his pistol against the side of the Blowfish's blubbery head and then threw him backwards into his friend.

Jack picked up the fallen knife as the Blowfish tumbled to the ground. Beyond them, the two pitbullfrogs were getting excited by the violence.

One of the Blowfish yelled, 'Kill 'im!' and the frogs lurched down the alleyway towards Jack, fangs bared. As the nearest prepared to leap, Jack twisted, shooting from the hip. The beast was flipped backwards, spraying what little brains it had across the alley like a bad sneeze.

The other pitbullfrog let out a squeal of alarm and bounded away into the darkness.

'Shit!' exclaimed one of the Blowfish angrily. 'Those things *cost*, man! You lousy—'

Jack pointed the revolver at the Blowfish and it fell silent. But in that second Jack had taken his eyes off Kerko. Enraged, the Blowfish launched himself at Jack and they crashed to the floor in a heap.

Jack lost his grip on the Webley and suddenly the Blowfish's hands were around his neck, squeezing hard.

'Kill 'im, Kerko!' the other urged.

Jack swung the Blowfish over onto the pavement and butted him with savage force. There was a crunch of bone, and Kerko went limp.

The other thug leapt onto Jack's shoulders, but it was a clumsy attempt and Jack threw him off easily. The Blowfish hit the metal shutters of a nearby shop with a clatter but was otherwise unhurt.

Jack was on him straight away. He pulled him to his feet and then punched the Blowfish hard enough to send him staggering out into the street.

'You're pretty tough for a fish,' said Jack, grabbing him by the scruff. 'But I've been handling your sort for over a century now. Give it up, kid.'

'Go to hell!' spat the fish. 'Torchwood filth!'

He struggled and squirmed, swinging his fists. Jack, suddenly tired and angry with this piece of alien flotsam, pushed him roughly away. The thug stumbled out into the road and into the path of an oncoming truck.

It was a skip lorry, carrying a heavy load. The driver, thickset and bald, was talking on his mobile. Jack watched in mute horror as the truck's big wheels gobbled the Blowfish up in a single, crunching mouthful, chewed it to a pulp and excreted it from the rear axle. The remains were dragged along the road until there was nothing left but mangled clothes, bones and a long smear of blood.

The lorry carried on without stopping; the driver hadn't even noticed. Jack didn't know whether to be relieved or appalled. He watched the red tail lights turn the corner and then stood and got his breath back in silence.

Kerko was crawling out of the alley. There was blood dribbling from a split in his forehead where Jack had butted him.

'You murdering bastard,' gasped the Blowfish. He pointed at the long, wet stripe of gore on the tarmac. His voice was choking. 'That was my little brother!'

'It was an accident,' Jack said lamely. 'I didn't mean it to happen.'

Kerko climbed slowly to his feet. 'Yeah, sure. That's what Torchwood does, innit? Kill you and make it look like an accident, yeah?' He spat a gob of dark blood at Jack. 'Murderer!'

'OK, that's enough!' Jack grabbed the Blowfish and spun him around, slammed him up against the wall. Then he jerked one of his arms hard up between his shoulders. 'You're comin' in.'

The handcuff clicked on and Kerko snarled. 'Taking me back to your HQ? What for? Why don't you just kill me now?'

'That's not how I do things,' Jack growled.

'Tell that to my brother, arsehole!'

Jack pressed his lips close to Kerko's ear. 'It's too late for him. But it's not too late for you.'

NINE

Gwen sat at her workstation and shivered. *All this steel and concrete*, she thought, looking across the water at the mirrored tower rising up through the cavernous ceiling. *Half of Torchwood's funding must go on heating bills.*

The Hub was abnormally quiet. She could see Ianto watering the plants in the Hothouse; a dark, silent, ghostly shape beyond the glass and ferns and bottles.

She shivered again and stared at the old, complicated machinery contained in the base of the water tower. The mirror panels surrounding the Rift manipulator were covered in algae, and with the constant trickle of water it looked more like a botched plumbing job than a super-complex control system for a time and space anomaly.

It was Gwen's turn to monitor the Rift sensors. Torchwood's semi-organic computer system ran its own routine of checks and balances on the powerful temporal energies the Rift contained, but day-to-day data analysis required human consideration. She glanced at the photo stuck to her workstation, reaching out to touch it gently. No more Tosh. No more Owen.

And soon, no more anyone.

If this Undertaker's Gift thing was as bad as Jack thought, then the three of them were up against the end of the world. Again. What was it the Hokrala lawyer had said? *A world of suffering?*

Ianto stepped as quietly as a cat into the pool of light which surrounded her workstation. He stood as neatly as a cat as well, feet together, all tidy and groomed and contained. He carefully placed a fresh mug of coffee down on her workstation, making sure it was on a drinks mat. *Great*, thought Gwen. *He's watered the plants and now he's watering me. I am a plant.*

'Shouldn't you be checking on our guest in Cell One?' Ianto queried.

'Shouldn't you be checking that Hokrala writ?' she asked. She looked at him and smiled sweetly.

'Ah. Touché. Coffee took priority, I'm afraid. It usually does.'

'That's avoidance tactics.'

'Psychologists call it displacement activity. Finding other things to do instead of the ones we should be doing.'

Gwen nodded thoughtfully. She picked up the mug and sipped. 'Good coffee, Ianto.'

'Slow-roasted Arabica. It contains natural antioxidants. It should help.'

She looked up at him over the rim. 'Help with what?'

'Sometimes it's easy to slip into a poor frame of mind. In this line of work it's hard not to become morbid. Drink the coffee and immerse yourself in work. Does it for me.'

'O-kay.' Gwen sighed and ran a hand through her hair, keen to change the subject. 'Where do you think this Undertaker's Gift could be, then? Somewhere in or around Cardiff, allegedly.'

'How big is it, do you think?'

'How big does a temporal fusion device need to be? The size of a house? A car? A football?'

'A pinhead?' Ianto blew out his cheeks. 'We know *nothing*.'

'I've set the Rift scanners to detect the kind of energy signature the computers say would be indicative of a temporal fusion device,' Gwen said, tapping the keyboard array. 'It's got to be high-end alien tech, and it's got to give off some kind of signal, even if it's just a general power leakage…'

'Any luck?'

'Absolutely nothing.'

'Tried anything else? A radiatory numospheric scan may show up something unexpected.'

'Already tried it. Didn't show anything.' Gwen pursed her lips thoughtfully. 'I wonder if that's good or bad?'

'You mean the whole thing may be a hoax after all?'

'Or it could just be very, very well hidden.'

Before Ianto could reply, his earpiece alerted him to a call from Captain Jack. 'Ianto? I'm coming in and I've got company. Get a detention cell ready, will you?'

'Successful fishing trip?'

'You shoulda seen the one that got away.'

TEN

Kerko flew across the cell and hit the wall, hard.

Instantly he whirled around, fighting, but the door had already slammed shut and the sound of bolts being thrown echoed around the chamber.

He pounded on the door, but it was useless. He was trapped. Imprisoned.

Jack Harkness walked calmly around to the unbreakable transparent fourth wall of the cell and regarded the Blowfish coolly.

'So this is it?' Kerko blazed. 'A Torchwood dungeon!'

'This isn't a dungeon,' Jack said. 'It's a holding cell. We've got dungeons if you want 'em, though.'

Kerko spat at him.

Jack watched the yellow sputum slide down the plastic and shrugged. 'Missed,' he said.

'You kill my brother and I end up in the slammer,' the Blowfish snarled in disgust. 'How does that work? It's not fair. It's not justice.'

'Torchwood isn't an agency of justice,' Jack said. 'We're here to salvage any alien or anachronistic technology that comes through the Rift. Flotsam and jetsam from across time and space, washed up on our little patch of beach. Or as we like to call it, Cardiff.'

'Bah.' Kerko paced angrily around the cell.

'We try to keep the twenty-first century smelling – however slightly – of roses,' Jack went on, leaning casually against the wall. 'So we utilise, catalogue, store or destroy anything that doesn't belong here. Where do you think that leaves *you*, Kerko?'

'Shit creek.'

'You got it.'

Kerko scowled. 'You killed my brother, man. I'll get you for that.'

'Ain't gonna happen, pal.'

The Blowfish pressed his scarlet face against the wall, right next to Jack. His breath steamed against the plastic. 'I'm gonna kill you. That's a promise!'

'Y'know what I hate, Kerko? The smell of bad fish. The sooner we get you into the freezer the better.'

'Up yours.'

Jack tapped on the glass. 'I'll be back soon to ask you some questions. Hope for your sake you've got some answers.'

And then he turned and walked away, leaving Kerko to smash his fists against the cell walls and scream for revenge.

Jack walked along the row of empty cells until he came to the last one. Gwen was standing in front of it, arms folded. She turned to look at him.

'Blowfish hoodies? *Really?*'

'Better believe it. One ended up under a truck, though. Messy. Kerko back there is understandably upset. It was his brother.'

'Oops.'

Jack arched an eyebrow. 'So when did you get so callous, Mrs Cooper?'

'I can't stand Blowfish,' she replied. 'Give me a Weevil any day – at least you know where you are with them. They don't have an attitude, just bad breath and big teeth.'

'Along with an insane urge to bite your head off. Some would call that attitude.'

'Yeah, but they don't *argue* with you.'

Jack laughed. 'Thing is, we've run right out of Weevils.'

'Still no sightings?'

'Nothing for the last fortnight. It's like they've just disappeared – or gone underground. I mean, *deeper* underground.'

'There must be a reason for that.'

'Could be anything. Right now I'm just glad we're not having to spend time rounding Weevils up.'

Gwen pursed her lips, considering. 'What are you going to do with your Blowfish, then?'

'Well, short of having him stuffed and mounted – please, no jokes – freezing is about our only option.' Jack frowned. 'I want to question him first though, when he's had a chance to cool off.'

'What about?'

'Recent Rift activity. Kerko's one of the few things to come through in the last couple of weeks that we can actually communicate with. There's been lots of stuff and a fair few aliens, but…'

'You mean like our friend in Cell One?' Gwen nodded her head at the nearby cell. 'Mr Quiet.'

Inside the cell was a large blob of orange-coloured jelly, roughly humanoid in shape but transparent, and with no discernible features, organs or clothes. It sat, silent and unmoving, on the concrete bench opposite. If it had any eyes then they would probably be staring at the floor. It had been in the cell for the last seven days and hadn't moved. It didn't appear to need any food or sleep but it was quite obviously alive. The glutinous mass which made up its body shifted occasionally as a thick bubble of some kind of gas oozed slowly around inside it.

Torchwood had stumbled across the creature on a building

site. Two workmen had died when they had poked the thing with their shovels – the jelly appeared to be electrically charged to a lethal degree.

Dressed head-to-foot in rubber – and probably not for the first time, thought Gwen wryly – Jack and Ianto had manoeuvred the creature to the Hub and led it, completely unprotesting, to Cell One. And there it had stayed ever since.

'Still no response?' Jack asked.

'Nothing,' Gwen shook her head. 'Just a big, fat zero. Not a word or a peep or a squeak. I'm not even sure it *can* make a sound. Maybe it's mute. Maybe it only communicates by telepathy, but I've run an ESP scan on it and it just doesn't register, so it's unlikely. I've tried talking to it, shouting at it, whispering, singing, signing, playing music, tapping, even reading the *Daily Mail* out loud, everything… But no reaction. It just sits there like a… like a great big jelly.'

'Marmalade,' said Jack. 'Ianto reckons it looks like it's made from orange marmalade.'

'Shredless,' Gwen agreed. 'Shredless marmalade that carries a 50,000-volt electrical charge.'

'Hey – maybe that's what we should call it: Marmalade.'

'Nope. I had a cat called that. Besides, Ianto wants to call it Eja.'

'Eja?'

'E-J-A. Electric Jelly Alien. Cute, don't you think?'

'He is, but the name isn't.' Jack tilted his head to one side, watching the strange, silent creature. 'Anyway, I think I prefer your idea.'

Gwen was puzzled. 'My idea?'

'Zero. As in we know zero about it; it tells us zero; and the chances of anyone surviving contact with it are zero.'

They stood in silence for a few more moments until Jack cleared his throat. Gwen looked questioningly at him. 'How are you, Gwen?' he asked, with only slight hesitation.

'Fine. Why?'

'Missing Rhys?'

'Of course. But at least the flat is tidy.'

He smiled. 'How's the Glock?'

Gwen raised an eyebrow, not expecting the question. 'It's OK. Good. Light weight, which is a bonus. Smooth. Easy to handle. Laser sights work OK. Ianto says he wants me to try it with some different ammo. Hollow points, thermium impact rounds, that kind of thing. Why?'

'I want to make sure we're all armed all the time right now.'

For the first time Gwen noticed that Jack's Webley was in its holster. He never usually carried his gun in the Hub. 'Worried about the assassin?'

'I need to know that when it really counts we can all do the job.'

Gwen blinked. 'You mean with a gun? You know I can.'

'Sometimes it ain't that easy.' Jack took a deep breath. 'Sometimes it isn't in the heat of the action that you have to do it. Sometimes you've gotta look the enemy right in the eye when you pull the trigger.'

'I know.' Gwen frowned. 'What's this all about, Jack?'

'It's about being able to make the right choice. Between life and death. I need to know that we can all do that when it really matters.'

Gwen stared at him. Her eyes were big and deep and black, just like they had been in the dream.

ELEVEN

'Hey, Ianto. Anything on that writ yet?'

'Still working on it.' Ianto looked up from a workstation and his eyes narrowed as he watched Jack sweep across the Hub. 'Is that a tear in your coat sleeve?'

Jack looked down at his arm and fingered the thick grey material of his greatcoat. There was a short, rough slit next to his elbow. 'Knife cut,' he said, shrugging. 'Blowfish fancied himself in a fight.'

'Leave it with me,' said Ianto with a tut. 'I'll fix it.'

Gwen followed Jack into his office. 'What's got into you, Jack? You've not been the same since the Greenway funeral.'

'Leave it.' Jack threw his coat down and slumped into the seat behind his desk. It overlooked the rest of the Hub via a large circular window. He stared out of it, pointedly not looking at Ianto, who was quietly and neatly carrying on with his work.

'No.' Gwen folded her arms. 'I won't leave it. All that business about making a choice – whether we could look someone in the eye and kill them. If you meant could *I* shoot someone in cold blood, then I'm not sure I could. It depends. It's a decision you can only make at the time.'

'I just want to make sure we're all on the same wavelength, that's all.'

'You mean that *I'm* on the same wavelength. Or don't you trust Ianto to make the right choice either?'

'I trust both of you. You know that.'

'Really? Then why did you go after those Blowfish alone?'

'There were only two of them and they were just kids. Didn't seem worth risking everyone.'

'Just yourself, you mean.'

'Not the same kind of risk. You know that.' He blew out a sigh and sat back. He folded his arms, mirroring her. He looked at her for a long time and then broke out a grin.

'Not working,' Gwen stated. She leaned on the desk. 'Just tell me the truth, Jack. What's the matter? What's worrying you? Is it the Undertaker's Gift?'

He had the decency to blink. The brilliant blue of his eyes looked steely now as the shutters came down, but she'd got him. Sometimes Gwen could really get under his skin.

Jack sat back, thinking what to say. Gwen waited. It was basic police interview stuff – let the silence do the work; people could never stand the silence. They felt compelled to fill it.

'I'm losing too many people, Gwen,' he said at last. He spoke very quietly. 'Too many.'

'So – what's the plan? You take all the risks because you can't be killed, and leave us to do the office work?'

'How many more people do I have to lose, Gwen? Tell me that. When's it going to stop?'

'You know it's not going to.'

'And how much more can I take? How many more deaths are gonna pile up in my memory? I'm running out of room in here.' Jack tapped the side of his head. 'Something's got to give.'

Gwen thought for a moment. She wasn't used to seeing Jack distraught. He was trying his best to hide it in that slightly cocky, slightly old-fashioned way of his, but she still felt her heart aching for him. Immortality had its price. 'Maybe,' she said carefully, 'you just need a break.'

'There aren't any holidays in this job. You know that.'

'Everyone needs some downtime.'

'The Rift never takes a break. Right now it's busier than ever. And, yes, we've got the Undertaker's Gift to deal with on top of that – *maybe*. We can't afford to stop. *I* can't afford to stop.'

'We managed without you for a while before.'

'That was different. And there were more of you then.' Jack turned and let his gaze rest on the back of Ianto's head as he worked at his station. 'I just can't bear the thought of losing you. Either of you.'

'If this Undertaker thing is real then you may be losing everyone – not just us.' Gwen sat on the edge of his desk and smiled at him. 'Besides, not even Captain Jack can do this job all by himself.'

'You'd be surprised,' he said, with a sad smile of his own. His eyes were staring into the past. Maybe even to a time before she had been born.

'If there *is* a temporal fusion device buried somewhere in Cardiff,' Jack began, 'then we are truly staring into the abyss, Gwen. If it's activated, then the chain reaction will destroy everything and everyone. The lifetime of this planet could be measured in hours, minutes, seconds and I can't do a damn thing about it.'

Gwen swallowed. 'Will it be quick?' she asked quietly.

He shook his head. 'No.'

TWELVE

Ianto called it the Hokrala Document.

It was a fairly ordinary-looking letter, until you inspected it really closely.

On one side, beneath the Hokrala corporate logo, were several lines of alien script. The markings looked like a series of tiny, jagged dots and dashes and slashes, all tied together in endless knots, varying in size and boldness. Which was probably what English looked like to aliens, Ianto guessed.

Ianto was about to scan the letter into the translator when he noticed something that made him raise the letter up to the light of one of his monitor screens.

A watermark.

It wasn't the Hokrala logo. This was an altogether different symbol: it was like nothing Ianto had ever seen before, or wanted to see again. A weird, convoluted design that reminded him of a Celtic knot, although there was something distinctly biological about the design, and something utterly violent. He tried turning the paper this way and that in the light, but he couldn't make any real sense of the mark at all. All he knew was that it left him feeling slightly queasy.

He was feeding the document into the translator machine as Jack and Gwen came out of the office.

'How's it going?' Jack called over. 'What's that bad boy got to tell us?'

'Maybe we'll just get away with a fine,' said Gwen, and Jack smiled dutifully.

The Hokrala Document was held beneath a transparent plastic screen. Above it was a monitor unit with a number of words all jostling around into position, as if they were hurriedly trying to line up for an inspection.

'This is the computer's best guess at a translation,' Ianto said. 'The programme is based on a series of interpolative linguistics algorithms that—'

'It's a covenant,' said Jack tersely. He tapped the screen as a series of words assembled. In the light of the workstation his face looked drawn and white. 'An agreement if you like, or an arrangement…'

The words kept shifting as the computer tried to assimilate the alien language and suggest the appropriate corresponding words in English. Sometimes it failed to settle on a word and the letters kept fluctuating.

'Who with?' Gwen asked.

Jack's finger traced a line. 'It says here: the Supreme Powers.'

'Supreme Powers?'

'That's what it says.'

'And who or what are the Supreme Powers?'

'I've no idea, but they sound kind of important.'

'It could be a translation glitch,' suggested Ianto. He rattled a few keys. 'It could simply refer to an umbrella organisation, perhaps – the body which controls Hokrala Corp?'

'Maybe,' said Jack flatly. He pointed at another section. 'What's that say?'

Ianto peered closer as the letters jiggled around and the words danced in and out of sense.

'Unbounded... unending... No – limitless. Erm... vengeance. Retaliation. Retribution.'

'Limitless retribution?' Gwen echoed.

'Not a fine, then,' said Ianto.

Gwen pointed at the translator screen. 'Wait a second. Look. It goes on... It's more specific: it's a warning. Is that "murder"? It moved too quick.'

Ianto tapped some keys again and squinted. 'No, it's "assassination". Oh. Your conman friend was right after all, Jack. They *are* sending an assassin to kill you.'

Jack straightened up. 'That just doesn't make sense.'

'True – you can't assassinate someone who's indestructible,' Ianto agreed.

'Actually, I was thinking that there's no one who could possibly *want* to assassinate me, but...'

'But surely it's impossible anyway, like Ianto says,' Gwen offered.

'Well, if someone was to teleport in here and shoot me with a focused solar-beam plasma rifle, then that could be tricky. How do I come back to life if I've been vaporised into a cloud of positively charged ions?'

'Could you?' Ianto asked.

'I really, really don't want to find out.'

'But could they actually teleport someone in *here*?' asked Gwen. 'Into the Hub?'

Jack pulled a non-committal face, trying on a smile that didn't seem as confident as usual. 'Well, we've got defences, but...'

'Nothing's foolproof,' finished Ianto.

'All right,' Gwen said, trying to sound confident and businesslike. 'At least we have a definite warning. They're out to get Jack. They're sending an assassin – possibly hiring some kind of hitman.'

'But why now?' wondered Ianto. 'Hokrala tipped us off about the Undertaker's Gift. If there *is* a temporal fusion device hidden in Cardiff, why would they have you assassinated? Surely they'd want you to try to find it and stop it.'

'Unless it's just a decoy,' Jack mused. 'A distraction. Keep me off my guard, running around Cardiff like a madman looking for a non-existent Time Bomb. Then – pow!'

'I still can't help thinking it would take more than one man, even with a focused solar-beam whatever-it-was,' Gwen said.

'Could be a team,' said Jack.

'A team?'

'Yeah, I once had a whole squadron of execution robots sent after me.' Jack's brows furrowed. 'But let's not go into that. Things were very different then. And I came to an agreement with the robots anyway.'

'An agreement?' Ianto echoed, raising an eyebrow.

Jack grinned at the memory. 'What a night *that* was.'

Ianto's eyebrows dipped. 'With execution robots.'

'Well, the squad leader, really. Top of the range, touch-sensitive bearings and micromesh skin. A bit uptight, of course, but me and a can of Brasso soon taught him how to relax.'

'I think I've heard enough,' Gwen interjected.

Jack suddenly seemed to remember what they had been talking about. 'Anyway,' he said, dropping the smile. 'Execution squad, hit team, lone gunman – does it really matter? They wanna whack Captain Jack.'

'There is another explanation,' Ianto said. 'Hokrala said you're going to fail to stop the Undertaker's Gift. What if this is their way of guaranteeing that?'

'You mean they *want* me to fail?'

'Perhaps,' said Ianto, 'they need you to?'

'That's a nasty thought.'

'OK, until we get to the bottom of this I think you should be grounded,' Gwen told Jack.

'Grounded?'

'Confined to the Hub. As of now.'

'We need to protect you, Jack,' said Ianto. 'You'll be safer here.'

'But I'm indestructible,' protested Jack indignantly.

'As in unsinkable,' Ianto noted.

'That's right,' Jack agreed.

'Like the *Titanic*,' added Ianto.

'We don't know what Hokrala are capable of,' Gwen put in. 'And they seemed pretty certain you'll fail to stop the Undertaker's Gift.'

Jack nodded slowly. 'All right… There is stuff I can do here. I can stay busy.'

'I'm going to recheck the Rift monitors,' Gwen said. 'You can interview the Blowfish.'

Jack saluted. 'Yes, ma'am.'

Gwen smiled sweetly back at him and then turned to speak to Ianto. 'You need to make sure the Hub defences are working properly – especially the matter transmission screening.'

'Yes, of course.' Ianto nodded. He had picked up the Hokrala Document again, intending to fold it and store it, but something new caught his attention. He held the paper up to the bright desk light again to inspect the watermark. He turned it over and looked again, puzzled.

'That's odd,' he said. 'It's gone.'

'What has?'

'The watermark. This paper had a watermark before, I'm sure of it.'

'Fascinating,' said Gwen, 'but not urgent.'

Ianto shrugged, replaced the letter in its envelope, and left it on the desk. He stared at it a moment longer and shivered. He couldn't think why, but it made his skin crawl.

THIRTEEN

Ray was sitting with Wynnie on the hard metal perch seats in the bus shelter on Plas y Parc, huddled against the cold, blustery weather. They were waiting for a bus to take them back up towards Cyncoed, and hopefully retrace Ray's steps of the night before.

'You're determined to get to the bottom of this, aren't you?' Wynnie asked, wincing as another icy gust of wind battered the shelter.

'Too right,' said Ray.

'And to think I gave up a lecture on heterogeneous catalysis for this.'

Ray's mobile rang, filling the shelter with the tinny strains of 'Where Did All The Love Go'. She answered it awkwardly, glancing quickly at the display. 'Hi Gillian. How's things?' She looked at Wynnie and shrugged.

'Hey Ray.' This was Gillian's habitual greeting. 'Glad I've got you. Didn't want to text this, it's too *weird*. But you know the funeral cortège—'

Ray felt a deep shiver run through her guts. 'What did you say? How do you know about the funeral…?'

'Your *blog* of course, silly cow. *Someone's* got to read it! D'uh!'

Ray shut her eyes in relief. Of course! The stupid bloody blog!

'Are you listening?' Gillian's voice was excited.

'What? Yeah. Go on. The blog. Stupid, really.' Ray couldn't think why she was lying, but it came easily. 'It's nothing, really. Take no notice of it.'

'No, no, don't be *daft*. I was at the party, remember. You'd been drinking but you *definitely* weren't pissed. Not *that* much anyway. But it was the blog you see, I couldn't believe it when I read it. Is it true? Did you see it as well?'

Ray was suddenly tuned in, her mind cutting through the chatter to the one salient fact. 'What do you mean, "as well"?'

'I saw it too! I saw the funeral!'

'How?'

'After you left I came out for some air – it was really *stuffy* in that house, wasn't it? – and I ended up looking for you. I was worried that you'd get lost or something, and I felt a bit guilty that I'd left you to walk home on your own.'

'That's sweet.'

'Whatever. I tried to follow you and then I found this stupid funeral thing, full of these *horrible*, dirty-looking men. I mean, they were *awful*... Just like you said in your blog. Someone pointed it out to me, and I thought *oh my God* that's *them*—'

Wynnie was looking at Ray wonderingly. 'What is it?' he mouthed. 'What's going on?'

'Wait,' Ray hissed, and that was all Gillian needed.

'Are you *with* someone?' she gasped. 'Oh! It's Wynnie, isn't it! You're with *Wynnie*!'

Ray started to deny it, more out of a desire to hurry Gillian back to the point of her call than anything, but hesitated at the crucial moment. It was all Gillian, a seasoned gossip, needed.

'Oh, it *is* Wynnie,' she squeaked. 'Did you spend the *night* with him?'

'Of course I didn't! Now, look, Gillian, about the funeral—'

'You *so* did spend the night together! No *wonder* you wanted to get off so early!'

'It's not like that—'

'Oh, come *on*, Ray – you must know he's *mad* about you!'

'What?'

'He's *completely* mad about you. Anyone can see it. Poor boy practically *dotes* on you.'

Ray felt a flash of irritation and confusion. She could already feel her cheeks going red. 'Shut up, Gillian. I am not seeing Wynnie.'

Wynnie visibly flinched as she said this, and Ray felt awful. But her mind was in a complete storm now. 'Look, where are you, Gillian? Can't we talk properly? I'll meet you somewhere.'

Gillian sounded excited at the prospect of being able to extract all the juicy details. 'Right! Sure. You can tell me *all* about it then. Say, meet me at the Black House.'

'The Black House?'

Wynnie looked up sharply at this, started to say something, but Ray waved him to silence.

Gillian was still chattering. 'Yeah. That's where I saw the funeral thing. I'm on my way there now. Meet you there, right?'

'OK.' Ray closed the call and looked at her mobile until it went dark. She tried to collect her thoughts and failed utterly. Her head was swimming. Wynnie wasn't saying anything, just standing there looking at her. Waiting. Eventually she looked up at him and asked, 'What's the Black House?'

FOURTEEN

The Interview Room was a bare cell on one of the lower floors of the Hub. Entrance and exit was via a narrow doorway and a flight of concrete steps leading up into the Hub proper. It was cold and unyielding and had, in the past – long before Jack Harkness had taken over control of Torchwood Three – occasionally been the scene of torture and murder. There were stains on the floor that no one wanted to investigate too closely.

'See, I told you we had dungeons,' Jack said as he sat down on a wooden chair.

Kerko glared back at him across the small desk that separated them. His hands were on the table top, handcuffed.

Ianto stood in the corner, by the steps, looking immaculate and stern. Jack gazed at him for a long second and then pulled his attention back to the Blowfish.

'Go screw yourself,' said Kerko.

Jack smiled. 'We can make this easy or hard, Kerko. It's up to you.'

'You don't scare me, Harkness. None of you do.'

'I just want to ask you a few questions.'

'Like I said.'

Jack raised an eyebrow. 'Not in the mood, Kerko. So – what's it to be? Hard or soft?'

The Blowfish sneered. 'What you gonna do? Set pretty boy over there on me?'

'Ianto could get you looking clean and presentable in ten minutes flat. Do you really want me to turn him loose?'

Kerko glanced across at Ianto, unsure how to respond.

Ianto stared impassively back. He could almost have been a shop dummy. Jack noticed that he was sweating, even though the Interview Room was cold. Perhaps he was worried that Jack had meant what he said, and was trying to visualise Kerko in one of his three-piece suits and a silk tie.

'How did you get here, Kerko?' Jack asked after a minute had passed. 'Was it through the Rift?'

'No, I came in a flying saucer. Of course it was the Rift. You're so dumb.'

'Straight from Rigel 77?'

'No, we stopped at Swansea Services.'

'I'm not in the mood for jokes, Kerko. I've been to Rigel 77. I know what goes on there. It's a maximum-security rehab centre with such a bad rep the Shadow Proclamation had to shut it down with troops. Systematic abuse, drugs, torture, institutionalised violence. They did it all on Rigel 77. I know because I was there. Were you?'

Kerko gave a slight shake of his head, a denial to all intents and purposes, but Jack could see the wariness in the Blowfish's eyes.

'So you were a 77er.' Jack's eyes narrowed into fierce blue slits. 'What did they do to you, Kerko? Waterboarding? Electric shocks? Bore worms?'

'I don't want to go back there,' Kerko said quietly.

'No need to,' Jack said. His voice was low. 'We can do all that stuff here. I've got someone upstairs right now, firing up the mind probe. Gotta love that mind probe. Know what my success rate is? One hundred per cent. One hundred. Of those that survived of course.'

The Blowfish sat staring at the table top, unmoving, for nearly a full minute. Jack let the silence hang. He could sense the silent war raging in Kerko's head: give in, fight, play for time, or deny everything? He was calculating the results of each course of action with the instinctive, ruthless sense of self-preservation that characterised his kind. Eventually, without looking up, he asked, 'What do you want to know?'

'I want to know about the pitbullfrogs for a start.'

'What about them? They were just a bit of fun.'

'They're killers. Wild and unpredictable and full of God knows how many alien pathogens. I killed one but we need to find the other one, Kerko. Where's it likely to go? Any ideas?'

'How should I know?'

'We've had one confirmed sighting,' said Ianto. 'Police cornered an unidentified – and unidentifiable – animal in a garage near Splott. They had to bring in a dog unit to deal with it.'

Kerko looked intrigued. 'And?'

'Two Alsatians dead – necrotic inflammation from infected bites.'

'Huh.'

'I like dogs,' said Jack. 'I don't like pitbullfrogs. Where would it go, Kerko?'

He shrugged. 'Dunno.'

'You're not being very helpful, Kerko.'

'What have I got to gain? Or lose?' The Blowfish curled a wet lip and sat back in his chair, folding his arms. A little of the old spark had come back. 'You're stuck with me here, aren't you? You can't send me back. You either keep me here in your prison cell or kill me.'

'There's always the deep freeze,' suggested Ianto.

'Might as well be dead.'

'You want me to make you an offer?'

Kerko shrugged.

'How about I promise you that if you tell us what we want to know, I won't put you back in the same cell as our pet Weevil.'

'You've got Weevils here?' A smirk. 'Figures. They stink, eat crap and fight. Should fit in on this planet just fine.'

'It's not just the pitbullfrogs I'm worried about, Kerko. It's them, you, the guy in Cell One. We've even had Grolon rats swimming in the canals. Last week a load of them dragged an angler into the water and stripped him down to the bone.'

Kerko snorted. 'Never did like anglers.'

'Something's going on with the Rift,' Jack continued. 'We're being flooded with aliens, and *I wanna know why*.'

Kerko made no reply. He just sat and stared at the desk.

'Let me ask you another question,' ventured Jack. 'Have you ever heard of something called the Undertaker's Gift?'

'Up yours,' said Kerko.

'Weevil's waiting. And she's hungry. Maybe she fancies a fish supper, what do you think Ianto?'

'More than likely, I should say. I think I've got a bottle of Tartar sauce somewhere.'

Jack rewarded him with a tiny smile and then looked back at Kerko. 'Well?'

'Go screw yourself. I'm a 77er, remember, and you don't scare me. You killed my kid brother and I've got nothing to lose, so tell me what you *expect* me to do? Sit here and answer all your stupid questions or break your neck with my bare hands?'

And with this he launched himself across the table, fingers fastening around Jack's throat with sudden, wild anger. Such was the unexpected savagery of the attack that Jack found himself momentarily stunned, aware only of an agonising pain in his neck and a complete inability to breathe. Even handcuffed, Kerko had succeeded in getting a good, solid grip and his fingers were digging in like steel clamps.

Jack's chair crashed back as he struggled to his feet, teeth bared. Kerko was still holding him, locked onto him with a crazed strength forged from sheer, hard-as-iron hate. Jack tried to tear the Blowfish away but he just couldn't get the leverage. They gripped each other in a rigid dance of death until Ianto calmly stepped forward and pressed the muzzle of a stun gun against the back of Kerko's neck.

Pow.

The fish dropped to the floor without a sound and lay there, trembling as the electric charge dissipated through his nervous system.

Ianto picked up the fallen chair and helped Jack into it. 'You took your time,' Jack complained hoarsely, rubbing his throat.

'The stunner was in my pocket. I had to get it out, check the charge, take off the safety catch, aim it and pull the trigger. That all took a good three seconds. Sorry.'

Jack waved the excuse away. He found it difficult to speak and his mouth tasted like he'd been sucking batteries.

'Just sit there and get your breath back,' Ianto advised.

'I took the charge too, you know,' Jack complained. He felt suddenly, ridiculously old, and he knew it would be a minute or two before he recovered properly.

'Well, there I did have to be careful,' admitted Ianto. 'I set the voltage to disable Kerko but not you.'

'Really?'

'Yes. Fish are more susceptible to electric shocks than humans.'

'Is that a fact?'

'Well, more of an educated guess, actually. But I'll check it for you later if you like.'

'Don't bother.' Jack forced a grin. 'Three *seconds*, huh? Not bad.'

'What do you want done with him?' Ianto nodded at the fallen Blowfish. A dark stain had spread across Kerko's pants where the surge of electricity had scrambled his autonomic reflexes and caused his bladder to void.

'Back in his cell,' Jack said. 'And don't clean him up.'

FIFTEEN

It was just starting to rain again as Ray and Wynnie got on the bus. It was full, so Ray ended up sitting a couple of seats away from Wynnie.

Her mind was in a whirl as the bus rumbled away from the stop. She couldn't look out because the windows had steamed up with all the damp passengers crowded inside and she found her gaze resting on the back of Wynnie's head.

He dotes on you.

To her amazement, Ray found herself looking at Wynnie properly, perhaps for the first time. He wasn't good-looking, not a bit of it, but you couldn't honestly say he was ugly either. He was a bit funny-looking, actually, Ray realised. His ears stuck out through the blond dreadlocks, and his face was a bit too long and angular. But there was something about Wynnie, something beyond what he looked like, that made Ray feel relaxed and happy in his company. But she didn't fancy him. She couldn't fancy him.

Wynnie looked around, sensing her attention, and smiled.

She looked away, forcing her mind onto other things. The funeral cortège. Gillian. What was it all about? What had Gillian seen? Could it really have been the same thing that Ray had witnessed? How could it have been?

A mile or so further on and the bus had emptied a little, and Wynnie came to sit next to Ray. 'Not far now,' he said. 'Next stop.'

'You definitely know where this Black House place is?'

'Yeah. I thought everyone did.'

'I'm not a local, remember.'

'I know, but we try not to hold that against you.'

'So what is this Black House thing anyway? A pub?'

'No way. I think it used to be a church, or part of one, a long time ago. You can still see where the graveyard was, but I think the actual building is empty or demolished.'

Ray shivered. Her vision had suddenly filled with a memory of the church she had glimpsed through the trees last night, where the funeral cortège had been. Could that have been the Black House?

Then she remembered the casket. And what was *inside* the casket.

Stop. Don't even think of it.

'Do you think it's got something to do with your visions?' Wynnie asked.

'They're not visions!' A couple of people looked up sharply at this, and Ray hastily lowered her voice. 'They're *not* visions. I *saw* that funeral cortège. I saw the pallbearers and a… coffin or casket. *I saw them.*'

'But there's no cemetery at the Black House, not any more. Why would a funeral cortège go there?'

'Don't ask me. But that's where Gillian says she saw it and that's where she's meeting us.'

'OK.' Wynnie rang the bell and stood up. 'This is our stop. Come on.'

They got off the bus and stood in the rain for a minute. Wynnie fiddled around with the collar of his jacket until he had managed to extract the foldaway hood. He put it up and tightened the drawstring. Ray didn't know whether to be ashamed of him or sorry for him. But she found herself grinning at him from under her beanie regardless, and he smiled back at her, not in the least bit embarrassed.

'So,' Ray said when the bus had left and they were alone. 'Where is this Black House, anyway?'

'This way.' Wynnie stepped over a gutterful of brown water and crossed the road. Ray hurried after him, following his brightly coloured rucksack. They passed some dilapidated houses with scrubby front lawns and no one home. They looked deserted, maybe even ready for demolition.

'Hey, I think I do recognise this area,' Ray said after a while. They were trudging along the side of a small park or something, surrounded by old, bent railings scabbed over with rust. 'From when I was lost after the party. It's around here that I saw the church and the cortège, I'm sure of it.'

'Makes sense, I suppose.' Wynnie located a gap in long row of railings where the metal spurs were missing. He ducked through and, after a moment's hesitation, Ray followed.

'I feel like a kid again,' she said. 'I used to sneak out of school at dinner time for chips. There was a gap in the railings there too.'

'Watch your step here,' Wynnie advised, pointing down. 'It's a bit overgrown.'

The undergrowth was thick and tangled, full of discarded rubbish. Ray now realised that Wynnie was dressed perfectly for the occasion: waterproof anorak, cargoes, heavy boots. He probably had a torch and first-aid kit in that stupid rucksack. But what had she come in? Trainers, skinny jeans and a denim jacket. Her only concession to the bad weather was one of Wynnie's Kasabian beanies and a pair of fingerless woollen gloves. Wonderful. Way to go, Ray.

She followed him across a patch of waste ground, stumbling

over an uneven surface littered with stones, weeds and big grey puddles. Up ahead there was a gang of dark, leafless trees waiting for them. Beyond the trees was a wide expanse of nothing but overgrown thistles and stiff, razor-sharp grass.

And then there was the church.

It was old, cold and forgotten. The windows were empty, there was no roof, and the walls were cracked and sprouting weeds.

'This used to be the cemetery,' explained Wynnie. There was evidence of where the cemetery walls had once stood – sections of low, crumbling black brickwork at various angles.

'What did they do with the graves?'

'They probably moved the recent ones. They can do that, with the right permissions and so on. That would've been back in the 1960s anyway. Ancient history.'

'And the older ones?'

Wynnie shrugged. 'Too deep, probably. Too decayed. They used to dig a lot deeper than six feet in the olden days, you know. And then there's subsidence, where the ground moves and squashes everything. Wooden coffins will have rotted and split. What's left of the bodies will have putrefied.'

'There is such a thing as too much information, you know.'

As they wandered through the trees, Ray's foot hit a large, square stone. Pushing back the undergrowth, she found what could have been part of an old gravestone. She was walking over someone else's grave – so why did it feel like someone was walking over hers?

The rain had stopped and there was a thin mist rising up from the ground. Ray headed for the remains of the church. 'So that's the Black House, is it?'

'What's left of it, anyway.'

The sense of neglect was almost overwhelming, like a physical force. It made Ray want to run away and never come back.

'It's… horrid.'

Wynnie nodded wisely. 'It's no beauty spot. Small wonder no developer has ever bought the land. Who'd want it?'

Ray began to walk around the remains of the walls, tracing the perimeter of the building. 'There's no *life* here. Nothing. Look – even the weeds are dead.'

It was weirdly quiet, too; no traffic or birdsong or anything. Just the quiet whisper of the rain and the sound of her trainers as she picked her way through the thistles. It reminded her of last night, when she had stumbled across the midnight funeral taking place in deathly silence.

'There's something else missing, too,' noted Wynnie.

'What?'

'No Gillian.'

Ray looked quickly around. 'She did say to meet us at the Black House.'

'And yet…'

'Maybe she's over there,' Ray suggested, pointing. 'I thought I saw someone in the trees just then.'

A figure was approaching through the row of spindly black trees on the far side of the area.

But it wasn't Gillian.

'Hi,' called Wynnie, with a little wave. 'We're looking for someone.'

The man was tall, dressed in a ragged black coat with thin arms and dark gloves. His head was covered in a thick cloth, wound around like bandages, leaving only slits where the eyes should be.

To Ray, the sight was terrifyingly familiar and she felt a surge of cold, sickly fear. The figure raised one arm and slowly pointed at her.

It was all she needed to snap her out of her paralysis. She grabbed Wynnie by the arm and physically dragged him away, pulling him along with her as she ran back towards the railings.

'Run!' she gasped.

Wynnie was saying something but she couldn't hear what. All she knew was that they had to get away, had to get out of this awful, dead place. There were more figures, the pallbearers she had seen the night before, walking across the wasteland towards them. All of them were slowly raising their arms and pointing.

Ray held Wynnie in a grip so hard she knew it must be hurting. But she couldn't let go; she couldn't stop or even look back.

'*Run!*' she screamed.

SIXTEEN

Jack stood in his shirtsleeves and waistcoat, leaning against the concrete wall opposite Zero's cell. His neck was still smarting where Kerko's fingers had dug in like grappling hooks. Somehow he had mislaid his coat, too, and it was cold down here. He had a sneaking suspicion Ianto had whisked it away for repairs. It would be dry cleaned too, in all probability. That coat had been through a lot over the years and it still looked good. *Could be talking about me,* Jack thought.

He stared through the plastic at Zero. What was the alien thinking? Was he even thinking at all? It was impossible to tell.

Ianto appeared quietly at his side with a cup of coffee. Jack hadn't even smelled it coming.

'I've put the Blowfish back in his cell,' Ianto said. 'He'll probably come round in a few minutes.'

'Thanks.' Jack looked at Ianto. 'You look beat. Get some rest.'

'I'm fine.'

'Don't argue,' Jack smiled. 'I'm in charge. Get some rest and that's an order.'

'Aye aye, Captain.' Ianto turned to leave again, paused, looked back. 'I *am* all right, you know.'

'Yeah, I know.'

But he wasn't. Ianto looked pale and tired and there was still that sheen of sweat on his forehead. At other times Jack would have been mildly excited by that, but something was worrying him now. Ianto *never* sweated. At least, not without permission.

'I thought I'd go back through the Archives,' Ianto suggested, pausing by the steps. 'You said there had been rumours of the Undertaker's Gift for as long as you've been here. If I check the records, I may find something that can help.'

'Yeah, good idea. See what you can dig out.'

Ianto nodded and left, leaving Jack alone with his coffee and Zero.

Jack remembered bringing Zero in, shortly after they detected the Rift incursion. The alien had been strangely compliant, utterly silent, bereft of hostility but completely lethal. Jack had worn a protective rubber suit and a pair of thick, insulated gauntlets – the kind of thing he imagined power station workers wore to handle radioactive isotopes, or fire crews on warships used to avoid burns. They had protected him from the fierce electrical charge Zero carried like a plague and they were hanging up nearby right now. Jack could put the gauntlets on and walk into the cell and try to make the alien respond – push him or shake him or punch him or whatever, anything to get a reaction.

Or he could just go in without the gloves.

Take the charge.

What would happen then?

Jack had been electrocuted before. Four times, to be exact. Or was it five? It got difficult to remember, sometimes: he'd died so many times. And on at least one occasion the charge hadn't been lethal and he'd only suffered second- and third-degree burns. That had been painful for a long time but, as ever, he had recovered. Not healed – just returned to his existent state.

But Zero packed quite a punch: 50,000 volts at a rough guess. It would kill him, again, for sure. But for how long?

And why was he thinking like this? What was so fascinating about dying? He knew he couldn't do it, no matter how hard he tried. *Or could he?* Was there something out there that could finish him, draw a line underneath his existence? When would it ever end? When everyone he had ever known was dead? If the Undertaker's Gift is real, he thought, then I might finally be about to find out. If Earth is shredded in four dimensions by a temporal fusion device detonating in the Rift, would that be enough to finish him? Or would Jack Harkness still be here, living, waiting for an end that would never, ever arrive? Just *existing*?

Would he float away into space, stiff and frozen, rimed with ice, to drift into an eternity of blackness with only his memories for company?

Jack's hand moved towards the lock on the cell door. Perhaps if he opened it, Zero would react.

'Jack?'

He turned guiltily as Gwen stepped into the cell corridor. 'Jack?'

'What is it?'

'I've been looking into something on the net.'

Jack felt as if he had to haul his attention back out of a deep pit. 'What?'

'The Undertaker's Gift. I've done every kind of scan I can for a temporal fusion device and there's nothing showing up. If it's hidden then it's bloody well hidden. So I did an internet search on all things associated with undertakers and came across something interesting.'

'Hit me.'

'There's a student blog entry that talks about a night-time funeral procession in the middle of Cardiff.'

Jack raised an eyebrow. 'And?'

'The blog also mentions Torchwood.'

SEVENTEEN

Ray and Wynnie bolted to the gap in the railings and scrambled through in a tangle of arms, legs and rucksack. Wynnie stumbled, fell, swore, and Ray helped him up. Without a word, they sprinted together for another half a mile before both of them had run out of breath.

They leaned against a wall, panting hard. Ray's lungs were burning and Wynnie could barely speak.

'What… what…' he gasped, swallowing with difficulty. He pointed back the way they had come. 'It was them! The people you saw last night!'

Ray nodded. She literally couldn't speak. Her heart was banging away in her chest and she was beginning to realise how incredibly unfit she'd got. Not that she had ever actually been fit in the first place.

'I've never been so scared,' Wynnie began, and then, quite unexpectedly, he laughed. 'I mean…'

Ray looked at him, aghast. How could he find this funny? She looked back the way they had come, but there was no sign of any pursuit. She heaved a sigh and rubbed at her sternum; her chest was really burning. 'What's so funny?'

Wynnie was still chuckling. 'I haven't run like that since I was a kid.'

'I've never… run like that,' said Ray. 'Ever.' And then she started to smile too.

In less than a moment they were both laughing, guiltily choking back the noise because they knew that there was no way they should find this funny.

'It's nervous tension,' Wynnie giggled.

They clung to each other for a few minutes, slowly getting their breath back. There was no sign of pursuit. In fact, there was no one else at all nearby.

'Those were definitely the guys I saw last night,' Ray said at last. 'They creeped me out then and they did it just now, in broad daylight. They're just so… horrible. They make me feel dirty just seeing them.'

'Yeah, well, they're all done up like something from Halloween,' Wynnie observed. 'I bet they're having a right laugh at us now.'

'You think?' Ray sounded doubtful and Wynnie shrugged. Ray felt sure that the strange, dark figures were utterly bereft of any sense of humour. 'Do you think we should go back and look again? See if they're still there?'

'No way,' Wynnie said quickly.

'Wait a sec,' Ray said, reaching for her mobile. She opened it and speed-dialled Gillian. It rang a couple of times and then switched to her familiar voicemail response:

'Hi you're through to Gillian. I can't take your call right now, but if you're interesting enough I'll get back to you soon. Cheers.'

Ray flipped the phone shut. 'No answer.'

'Busy?'

'Gillian screens her calls – she'd pick up if she knew it was me calling. And besides, she's supposed to be waiting for us at the Black House.'

'If she saw those guys hanging around then she probably took off double quick, like we did.'

Ray frowned at the silent mobile in her hand. 'Then why hasn't she called to tell me that?'

EIGHTEEN

They convened in the Boardroom. Jack tried to keep the meeting informal by perching on the edge of the table. 'So, what we got?'

'OK,' said Gwen, sitting up. 'Here it is.' She used the remote control to bring up the internet blog entry on the main screen. Several words were highlighted: funeral, cortège, Torchwood.

Ianto peered at the screen. 'It's by a student at Cardiff University.'

'It seems the world and his wife and even their *kids* have heard of us now.' Jack had never liked Torchwood getting any kind of publicity.'

'A special force called Torchwood,' Ianto read out appreciatively. Then his lips curled down in distaste. '"Like the X-Files but in Cardiff". Huh. Dream on, Mulder.'

'I always thought he was quite a fox,' said Jack.

'Please,' Ianto said. 'Any more and my sides will split.' He nodded at the screen. 'Who are these people, really? The person writing the blog, I mean?'

Gwen called up an ID document on the screen – it was a Student Union card complete with photo of a pale, rather plain-looking girl with dark hair and heavy black eyeliner. 'The blog is written by one Rachel Banks, undergraduate. Born 16 April 1990, Leicester. Nothing special, nothing outrageous, nothing abnormal. Parents split up when she was thirteen, dad went out to work in Dubai, she lived with her mam in Bristol. Came to Cardiff to study Ecology, but according to her course tutor is likely to switch to Zoology at the end of the year. Staying in digs in Colum Road.'

'And Wynnie?' prompted Jack.

'Meredydd-Wyn Morgan-Kelso,' said Gwen, flicking the remote. A different Student Union ID pass came up on the screen. This one showed a picture of a tall, thin lad with unkempt blond hair, facial studs and rather soft brown eyes. 'Born 24 November 1985, Hengoed. Nothing special, nothing outrageous, nothing abnormal – unless you count an abiding interest in Heavy Metal, comics and a post-grad research position at Cardiff School of Chemistry – he's currently completing an MSc in Catalysis. And, of course, there's his name. Bit of a mouthful, hence "Wynnie". I think it's rather nice.'

'What do you call a double double-barrelled name?' wondered Ianto.

'Quadruple-barrelled?' Jack suggested.

'Whatever,' said Gwen. 'I'm guessing he's a mate, boyfriend, it doesn't matter. But he's the one who mentions Torchwood.'

'And what does he know about us?'

'I doubt he knows anything. He's heard the name, that's all. He's a member of the university astronomy club, writes for the Union website and once subscribed to *Fortean Times*.'

'Uh-oh,' said Ianto.

'So where is all this leading us?' Jack asked.

Gwen smiled. 'I tracked Rachel Banks's online activity. Knowing she was a blogger it seemed likely that she uses the web for most things, including shopping. She bought a mobile phone last August and so I traced the number and the most recent calls.

She's in regular contact with Meredydd-Wyn Morgan-Kelso, but this morning she took a call from another student…' Gwen tapped the remote control a couple of times and a female voice with a strong Valleys accent filled the boardroom:

'*No, no, don't be daft. I was at the party, remember. You'd been drinking but you definitely weren't pissed. Not that much anyway. But it was the blog you see, I couldn't believe it when I read it. Is it true? Did you see it as well?*'

Rachel's voice: '*What do you mean, "as well"?*'

'*Well, I saw it too! I saw the funeral!*'

Jack's eyes narrowed and Ianto looked up sharply. Gwen used the remote to fast-forward through some more of the conversation. 'Hang on, there's some romance stuff next. I'll cut to the chase.'

Rachel Banks's voice crackled back: '*Look, where are you, Gillian? Can't we talk properly? I'll meet you somewhere.*'

'*Right! Sure. You can tell me all about it then. Say, meet me at the Black House.*'

'*The Black House?*'

Jack frowned and mouthed, 'The Black House?'

The Valleys girl was still chattering. '*Yeah. That's where I saw the funeral thing. I'm on my way there now. Meet you there, right?*'

'And there you have it.' Gwen killed the recording with the remote control. 'Rachel Banks and this Gillian person, both claiming to have seen the mystery funeral cortège in the early hours of this morning, and a location.'

'The Black House is an abandoned church near Cyncoed,' Ianto said. 'It was scheduled to be knocked down in 1966, ready for a redevelopment that never happened. There's nothing there now – just the shell of the church and waste ground. The developers pulled out unexpectedly and no one has ever taken it up.'

'I've already checked it for signs of Rift activity,' Gwen said. 'There are quite a few level-five temporal energy spikes in the area stretching over a two-week period, peaking last night. It looks like a definite winner.'

Jack didn't look convinced. 'These kids… they're just students. We've run into this kind of thing before. They invent stuff without even realising it. I once spent an entire summer running around trying to trace a suspected Golgothron gambling ring in the Old Brewery Quarter. Turned out to be the University First XV playing strip poker.' His eyes glimmered for a second at the recollection. 'I mean, don't get me wrong, that was an interesting case in its way… but not Torchwood business.'

'We can't ignore this, Jack,' insisted Gwen. 'It's the only possible lead we have.'

'It's really not much of one at all.'

Ianto held up a hand. 'And yet… there may be something in it.'

'What?' Jack demanded.

'I checked through some of the archive material.'

'And?'

'Nothing much in relation to the Undertaker's Gift or space-time fusion bombs,' Ianto said, 'but there was one case that caught my eye.' He opened the manila folder on the desk and took out some sheets of yellowed, typewritten foolscap paper. 'This is a report written in 1919 by Torchwood operative Harkness, J.' He glanced up at Jack. 'Looking good for your age.'

'It's all down to clean living,' Jack said.

'What's the report about?' Gwen asked.

'It's a missing person report – but there was a Rift angle and so it fell into Torchwood's jurisdiction. The country was still in a state of turmoil following the end of the First World War, and quite a number of soldiers, many horrifically injured, were trying to make a life in post-war Britain. There was little in the way of rehabilitation programmes. Some of the men were so badly wounded that they would never be allowed a place in normal society again – men with half their faces blown off, or no hands, or completely limbless. They were sent to stay in special hospitals, kept apart from the rest of the world because they were deemed to be too badly mutilated to be seen.'

'That's awful,' said Gwen.

'That's war,' said Jack knowingly.

'A disused church was converted into a hospice for some of these men,' Ianto continued, 'including 23-year-old Corporal Francis Morgan of the Welsh Fusiliers. He was injured at Ypres and sent home to recover. He went missing en route from France.'

'I remember that case now,' Jack said. 'Harriet Derbyshire had been looking into it. Torchwood took an interest because one of the guys Morgan was travelling back with made a statement to the police when he disappeared. He claimed this Francis Morgan had been abducted.'

'By aliens?' Gwen ventured.

'No such thing in those days,' Jack smiled. 'At least, not in the conscious mind of ordinary folk. No, but Morgan's pal said he'd seen the men who took him away.'

Ianto held up the foolscap report and read part of it out: '"It were unbelievable. But I saw it with my own eyes. I think they must have been gypsies – Romanies who fought with the French against the Hun. They were walking wounded themselves, I reckon. They wore ragged old clothes and their faces were all bandaged up, burned in all probability."' Ianto looked up at Gwen and Jack. 'Sound familiar?'

'It's the men Rachel Banks described,' Gwen realised, excited.

'It carries on,' Ianto said, tapping the report. '"They came in one night and took Frank away. He couldn't do much to resist, being in the condition he was, and I couldn't help him either. But I picked up my crutches and followed them out anyway. It was a bright, moonlit night and I could see it all quite clearly – even with one eye. They never said a word, those gypsies, but there were quite a few of them. They formed a procession, like a funeral cortège. It was very sinister, and it was cold, and I couldn't see what they'd done with Frank. I called out to them but they just ignored me, and then set off, slow-like, as if they were pallbearers at a burial. And then the weirdest thing happened. They just disappeared. Literally vanished into thin air. I wasn't seeing things. I might have lost a leg and I may be blind in one eye, but there's nothing wrong with my brains and I know what I saw."'

As Ianto closed the file, Jack said, 'No one ever saw Francis Morgan again.'

'But those men – the gypsy men, the pallbearers, whoever they were. They're exactly what Rachel Banks describes in her blog.'

'You're right,' Jack admitted. He thought for a second and then clapped his hands to signal the fact that he had come to a decision. 'OK. Gwen, Ianto, good work. Follow it up. Get yourself down to this Black House place and take a look.'

Gwen gathered her things together. 'On my way.'

'I'll stay in the Hub,' Jack said. 'I still want to work on our friend Zero, and then there's Kerko too. Plenty to do without sticking my head above the parapet for the Hokrala hitman.'

'I was going to carry on translating the writ,' Ianto said. 'There's something about it that bothers me.'

'No,' Jack said. 'You can go with Gwen.'

Gwen said, 'Honestly, Jack. I can manage on my own.'

'No, I want both of you to go.'

Gwen's stare hardened. 'We don't need to go everywhere in twos. I'll be fine.'

She turned to go, ending the discussion, but Jack wasn't finished. 'I said I want both of you to go.'

She stopped at the door. 'I can manage,' she said firmly.

'It's not up for discussion.'

She frowned now, with a spark of fire in her big, dark eyes. 'I beg your pardon?'

'I said I want you both to go. What harm is there in that?'

'I don't need my hand holding,' Gwen insisted. 'And neither does Ianto. At least, not by me.'

'It's not that…'

'Then what is it, Jack? Actually? Or do you just want us both out of the way? Is that it? Are you expecting an assassin to materialise any minute and you want us both safely out of harm's way?'

'I'm not arguing about it, Gwen.'

'Well I am!' And with that she turned on her heel and strode away.

Ianto looked questioningly at Jack.

'Go with her,' said Jack. 'That's an order.'

NINETEEN

Jack watched on the CCTV in his office as Gwen's blue Peugeot pulled out of the underground garage. She had used her own car and not the SUV, just to make the point. Headstrong and independent and as gorgeous as hell. Jack could picture Ianto in the passenger seat, gripping the armrests tight as Gwen hurled the Peugeot along in quiet fury. Jack smiled and shook his head. 'Gotta love the woman.'

The Hub was empty at last, silent save for the muted click and whirr of the computers and Rift manipulator. Jack sat quietly for another minute, recalling the mud and fear of the trenches at Passchendaele, where he had fought in 1917. He could still smell the mustard gas and hear the echo of the guns, the incessant barrage of the twenty-pounders, day and night, churning the countryside into mud. So many men died that the mud became thick with corpses, and every field gun barrage would mix the flesh and bones up with the mud again. They had ended up digging trenches where the walls were lined with the severed limbs of fallen comrades. It was the stuff of nightmares, something he would never forget.

Nightmares.

Jack never really slept, but he did sometimes close his eyes and rest. He could zone out, empty his mind, reach a deep state of meditation that served him as well as sleep.

Sometimes he dreamed, and sometimes the dreams were bad ones.

If he shut his eyes now, a vivid picture formed in his mind: a cold, desolate graveyard. The ghost of an old church looming through the mist. He didn't know where the image came from or why, but something was putting it there. He had told Ianto that it was possible to become so attuned to a place, an environment, that one could actually sense when things weren't right. With a time rift so close, and with Jack's history of time travel, it meant that he was sometimes almost preternaturally aware of the subtle changes in his surroundings.

He knew something bad was coming. Real bad. He couldn't identify what it was, or what form it would take, but he felt as though he was standing on a precipice, overlooking the destruction of the world. And it started here, with him.

And Gwen.

He could see her in the graveyard, walking away from him, looking back over her shoulder and smiling. She wanted him to follow her.

He couldn't move. He was paralysed, unable to even speak. She laughed at him then, lightly, musically, amused by his plight.

She sauntered through the cemetery, running her fingertips over the gravestones.

There were other people with her now – tall, emaciated figures in shabby funereal clothes, faces blanked by old, stained bandages.

Gwen walked across to one of them and they embraced. Jack wanted to scream, but he couldn't even move. He felt the tears welling in his eyes as Gwen held the pallbearer's head, kissing him deeply. And everywhere around, Jack now realised, there were corpses. He was surrounded by them, knee deep in cold, unmoving bodies. That's why he couldn't move. When he looked down at the nearest body, Jack saw that it was Ianto – his face was white and stiff, his mouth open and his eyes dry beneath waxen eyelids.

Gwen was laughing again, glancing back at Jack to check he was still looking at her. She kissed the pallbearer again, his top hat falling to the ground as they worked their tongues.

With a gasp, Jack opened his eyes and found himself back in his office. He had allowed the dream in again. He had to concentrate, resist it, focus on what had to be done.

Something bad was coming and he had to be ready.

TWENTY

Jack crossed the Hub and went straight to the armoury, letting himself in through the triple security lock with cool efficiency. Inside were racks of weaponry gathered from across the globe and various times and places.

He picked a pair of heavy SIG Sauer 9mm pistols, Torchwood-customised to take a variety of ammunition and fitted with laser sights. He took an energy lance, a Sontaran Stenk 11 pistol and a pair of AI throwing knives. He dumped the whole lot in a canvas bag and then, almost as an afterthought, picked up a fresh box of .38 shells for his Webley.

He hauled the bag down to the firing range, a disused underground railway tunnel that had long ago been blocked off and converted into a shooting alley. Jack often came here when he was feeling tired, or confused, or just plain angry. Firing off a few rounds always helped, and, even if it didn't, aiming a gun was a perishable skill that had to be practised.

If someone was going to come for him, even down here in the Hub, his base, his *home*… then he would be ready. He would stand and fight.

He warmed up the SIGs first, stripping them, loading them

and firing them with easy, familiar movements. Mostly Jack stuck with his tried and trusted Webley service revolver. But he had led a life that had familiarised him with many different weapons through the years and he was as comfortable using a state-of-the-art semi-automatic like the SIG as he was with a First World War British Army officer's pistol.

At the end of the tunnel were some targets – cardboard cut-outs of Weevils, Blowfish and sundry other hostile aliens. Some of the targets were human. The trick was to avoid hitting those.

The 9mm slugs tore chunks out of several Weevils and practically decapitated a Blowfish. It was good shooting, though, and strangely satisfying. He put the SIGs down when they grew too hot to handle properly. He tried the energy lance but it incinerated not only half the targets but several human cut-outs as well. Perhaps not.

The Sontaran gun wasn't much better. Too powerful, too brutal, short, ugly and nasty – just like its original owners. Still, it had its uses and was more controllable and easier to use than the energy lance.

The AI knives were more fun. They were passive-telepathic trintillium blades forged with microscopic internal nano-gyros which could alter the knife's passage mid flight. You could throw them in almost any direction, but so long as you knew exactly where you wanted them to go they'd find the target. Ideal throwing-knife if your target was hiding around a corner. They took a bit of practice and controlling, but eventually Jack could throw one of them the length of the gallery and let it come back to him, flipping over and over, so that he caught it by the handle. OK, so he nicked his fingers a few times but that was one of the advantages of being immortal: the cuts healed up in minutes.

He stowed the knives and, finally, drew the Webley from its leather holster at his waist. It felt heavy and comfortable in his hand, the wooden grips worn smoothly into the shape of his palm after so many years of use. The gun boomed satisfyingly as he fired, the huge calibre bullets punching massive holes in the targets.

The sharp smell of cordite filled the air once more and a lazy wreath of gun smoke floated around the room. But Jack could only ever smell perfume down here; a lingering memory of a blissful couple of hours spent with Gwen Cooper in her first few days on the job. Teaching her how to shoot, up close and personal, his arms around her as he altered her stance, his hands on hers, tutoring her in every detail of aiming slowly and carefully, squeezing, not pulling, the trigger. Then how to shoot quickly, from the hip, from the holster, from the shoulder, one gun, two guns, face-on, side-on, crouched, rolling, laughing. He smiled at the recollection; happy times and places indeed.

It was funny, Jack thought, how time separated you from tragedy and allowed you to remember the good times rather than the bad. But what if, cumulatively, the bad times began to outweigh all the others? What if the times he had laughed at Owen Harper's caustic sense of humour were replaced by the memory of him lying on his back with a large, bleeding hole in his chest? Or the memory of the brilliant Suzie Costello was replaced by the sight of her face down on the jetty, pumped full of bullets but still not dead? Or the whole Torchwood team, pre-millennium, slaughtered by their leader Alexander Hopkins, driven mad by the responsibility?

There were people stretching right back through a hundred years that Jack could think of who were dead, and he could remember how each and every one of them had died. Had he become obsessed with death? The one thing he could never have, never experience, had become the driving force in everything he did.

One of the first times they had used the alien Resurrection Glove to bring a dead man back to life for just a minute or two had been on a murder victim in a rain-lashed Cardiff back alley. And Jack had used those precious, stolen moments of life to ask the man *what was it like? What was there? What was waiting in the darkness?*

The answer, of course, was: *you really, really don't want to know.*

And, gradually, Jack had come to realise that he genuinely *didn't* want to know. Because whatever waited there, in that undiscovered country, should remain undiscovered. It was dark and endless and utterly unforgiving. And it scared him – because although he may never encounter it, he knew the people he loved more than anything else *would.* They always did.

Ianto would die. He would slip out of Jack's arms for ever one day – into the cold, black embrace of death, never to return.

And Gwen. When Jack closed his eyes he could picture her lying on a mortuary slab, white as plaster. Those big, beautiful eyes would never open again, never see him, never understand him.

Something moved in the doorway to the firing range and Jack snatched the Webley up in one smooth, reflexive motion, his finger tightening on the trigger as he stared down the hexagonal barrel at the intruder.

'Hold it right there,' said Jack, his voice steely.

TWENTY-ONE

Ianto slowly raised his hands. 'Don't shoot,' he said. 'I'll come quietly. Or loudly. Whichever you prefer.'

Very gradually, Jack relaxed his trigger finger. It took a few seconds before he could speak, and he used the time to let out his breath in a long hiss.

'Ianto, you just came within a gnat's lick of getting a bullet between the eyes.' Jack lowered the revolver, gently easing the hammer back down with his thumb. He slipped the gun back into the holster and closed the flap. 'Don't ever do that again. You won't get a second chance.'

'Expecting trouble, I see,' Ianto remarked lightly. He still looked pale but that might have been shock.

'An assassin – remember?'

'Sorry to disappoint.'

Jack sighed and brushed angrily past him, heading for the exit. 'I thought I told you – no, scratch that, I *ordered* you – to go with Gwen.'

'Yes, I know you did. But she really, really didn't want any company. And then my PDA picked this up.' Ianto held up his portable scanner. The screen was flashing an urgent blue. 'I set it to a random scan of all chronon-range wavelengths, linked to the main Hub sensors.'

Ianto led Jack to a workstation where he punched up a program on the screen. He hit another key and one of the screens filled with a jagged oscilloscope of readings that matched those on his PDA.

'What is it?'

'Some kind of signal.'

'Teleport?'

'No.'

'Communications?'

'Possibly.' Ianto's finger traced one of the more wiggly lines on the screen. 'It's on a multiple-phased wavelength on a very particular sub-ether frequency.'

'Just tell me what it is, leave the rest in the dictionary.'

'I've taken a series of measurements in the sub-ether series and the signal – if that's what it is – is right up *there*...' Ianto pointed at one of the peaks of the jagged line as it traced across the screen, '... in the active chronon range. Meaning there's a time element to it.'

Jack seized the implication straightaway. 'Has it detected a temporal fusion device?'

'I don't know.'

'So where's the signal coming from?'

'Somewhere in the Hub.'

Jack just looked at him. Ianto swivelled and pointed at another monitor, showing CCTV footage from the cell block downstairs. 'Cell One, in fact. Our mystery guest, Mr Zero.'

TWENTY-TWO

Gwen drove angrily but carefully. Now wasn't the time to have to explain herself to some over-eager traffic cop in a bad mood. It was easy with the SUV; the police knew what it was on the whole and left it alone. But her own car was different. It was ordinary. If *anything* could be ordinary in her life any more. Things were getting weirder and weirder, and, bizarrely, the strange and the exotic and the dangerous had now become the staple ingredients of Gwen's life.

Sometimes she had to really concentrate, just to work through the ordinary, boring, domestic routines. It was easy for Jack and Ianto, they lived for Torchwood. But Gwen had a life, a real life. A home and a partner and, possibly, plans for the future.

She didn't intend to die any time soon, that was for sure. Jack seemed intent on protecting her and Ianto, but she didn't need it. She'd faced some tough situations in the last couple of years but she was still here, still standing, and ready for more.

Gwen Cooper loved Torchwood.

She loved the excitement, the danger, the never-knowing-what's-coming-next. She loved the alien technology, the firepower, the friends she'd made and, above all, the knowledge that she had helped to make a difference. She'd saved lives – not just one or two but hundreds, if not thousands. She'd met people from space and people from the future and aliens and monsters and all kinds of shit – and she'd still done it with a home to run and a husband to care for.

And so sometimes she really had to concentrate, just to get the normal things done: shopping, meals, laundry, birthdays. Rhys was good but he had a job of his own and, at the end of a day, he was just a man. And men were useless at the routine, day-to-day domestic stuff. Unless they were Ianto.

Inevitably, her thoughts would always turn back to Torchwood matters. She was worried about Jack. Jack was taking too much on his shoulders. He wanted to protect everybody and the responsibility was overwhelming him.

She was worried about Ianto as well. He looked drawn and ill. Usually he was the very picture of health, but ever since the Hokrala situation had blown up he seemed drained and pale. But the workload *had* been intense in the last few months – there was too much for just the three of them to do, and Ianto worked so hard 'behind the scenes', as Jack liked to put it, to keep the Hub and Torchwood running as smoothly as possible.

Gwen pulled the Peugeot over to the kerb and parked near some railings. She was in the vicinity of the Black House. She zipped her jacket up as she got out of the car. The sky was cold and grey and it looked like more rain was on its way. The clouds hung over the city like a threat.

It was a strangely quiet and deserted area. There was an atmosphere: oppressive, dismal, unsettling. Gwen shivered. It was lonely here. There was an absence in the air that was almost tangible, as if Gwen could reach out and grab a handful of nothing, and feel its cold, unforgiving emptiness.

Wrapping her arms around herself, she headed towards the Black House.

TWENTY-THREE

Ianto pointed the handheld PDA scanner at Zero and checked the reading.

'Still nothing.'

Jack bared his teeth in frustration. He was leaning against the cell door, arms folded. 'I just don't get it.'

'The signal's definitely coming from here,' Ianto insisted. 'From him.'

The amorphous orange creature sat impassively on the bench, where it had remained ever since its arrival. It seemed to glow with a faint, inner luminescence, casting a strange marmalade light around the interior of the cell. Bubbles oozed lazily through the jelly as Ianto tried another scan and Jack glared at it.

Ianto shook his head in confusion, his face bathed in the vibrant blue light of the scanner. 'I'm relaying the readings from the Rift monitors through the PDA. They definitely register activity in the chronon range. There's some kind of time displacement – or at least distortion – around the creature. It's tiny, minute even, but it's absolutely there. And it's regular, sequential... definitely a signal. It's got a rhythm.'

'The blues,' said Jack suddenly. 'That's what it's got.'

Ianto looked at him. 'As in Rhythm and Blues? As in R 'n' B?'

'It's more than a signal, Ianto. It's a cry for help.'

Ianto looked back at Zero, who simply sat there, unmoving. 'Help from us?'

'I don't know.' Jack moved to the window, squatting down so that his eyes were roughly level with the creature's head. 'That's no bomb. It's alien, it's lost, it's a long, long way from home. It's come through the Rift and it can't even communicate with us. It can't even touch us.'

'It packs a 50,000-volt charge. It's probably scared to touch *itself*.'

'No, no, listen.' Jack stood up, his eyes and intense blue. 'What if it's keeping still as some kind of defence? Like a lizard when it thinks it's been seen – it freezes, still as a statue. Hopes the prey doesn't notice it and walks on by.'

Ianto looked sceptical. 'It's sitting there in Cell One thinking, "If I keep still and don't move a muscle, they'll never know I'm here"?' Meaning that it's not a bomb, just alien, lost and incredibly stupid?'

'I don't know. We may never know. Some things in the universe are just unknowable, Ianto. But ten gets you one that poor creature is scared half to death and just hoping to God that it can somehow get back home.'

Ianto looked sadly at Zero. 'It's going to be disappointed.'

'It's crying out for help – in a way we can't even understand, let alone hear. It's not ultrasonic, or telepathic, or anything we can register. But it's screaming, Ianto, and the Rift sensors are picking it up.' Jack gently spread his fingertips on the glass partition. 'And check it out now. Does it look different to you, since we brought it in?'

'Not really – it hasn't budged an inch. Well…' Ianto squinted at it, scratched his head, puffed out his cheeks. 'All right, maybe, just maybe, it's a bit thinner. Like it's lost weight.'

'Like it's looking more human,' Jack nodded. 'When we found

it, Zero was just a big blob of orange jello. By the time we got it back to the Hub, it looked like a rough approximation of a human – blobby, but bipedal. And look at it now – just a bit more human, wouldn't you say? The limbs are more defined, the head smaller.'

'It's trying to make itself look like us,' Ianto realised in a whisper. 'Gradually changing shape and structure to resemble a human being.'

'Camouflage. Trying to blend in. Another defensive measure? OK, it's not very convincing – it still looks like it's made from half a tonne of marmalade, but it's *trying*. It can't hope to copy us exactly because it's never encountered human beings before… But it can't help trying.'

And now when Ianto looked at Zero he saw something incredibly sad and pathetic – unknowable, but more lost and more forlorn than anything he had ever known before. And the little, oscillating zigzag on his PDA screen was a silent, sub-etheric wail of despair.

'What can we do?' he asked quietly, stepping closer to Jack.

Jack put his arm around Ianto's shoulders, pulling him closer. 'There's nothing we can do.'

And then the intruder alarms started clanging.

TWENTY-FOUR

The klaxons were still howling and warning lights strobed wildly as Jack and Ianto sprinted into the Hub.

'What the hell—' began Jack.

The alarm continued to whoop as Ianto shouted, 'The defence systems have detected an incoming matter transmission!'

In the centre of the Hub, something was materialising.

'Assassin!' realised Jack, already pulling his gun from its holster.

The fizz of energy coalesced into a man standing by the base of the water tower. He was tall and thin and dark and already turning to face them as Jack pulled the trigger on the Webley. The noise of the gunshot crashed around the Hub, and for a second everything seemed to freeze.

Ianto crouched, fumbling for his gun, a look of horror and fear on his ashen face.

Jack stood tall, erect, arm extended like a signpost to death. The revolver was held firmly in one hand, level with his eyes, which shone with a steely purpose through the smoke that swirled around his fist.

The man by the water tower threw his head back and his

arms out wide. The .38 had entered his chest, upper left, a heart shot. The bullet, travelling at over 225 metres per second and spinning like a drill bit, splintered a rib and punched a large hole right through the right ventricle. The metal tore open arteries, shredded veins and ripped a chunk out of the lung, before exiting between the man's shoulders in a dark splatter. He teetered for a moment and then fell backwards with a startled choke as the blood surged up his windpipe and out of his mouth.

He hit the metal floor with a heavy clatter and time began to flow once more.

Ianto ran over, automatic now drawn and aimed at the intruder in a two-handed grip, ready to deliver a kill shot to the head if necessary.

But Jack had skidded to a halt by the fallen man and now he fell to his knees with a gasp of despair. The man's features were alien – white-faced, narrow-eyed, with a dark mouth. Green, inky blood dripped onto the floor and a top hat lay discarded nearby, dropped the moment he had been shot.

'I don't believe it,' groaned Jack, looking up at Ianto. 'I've just shot Harold!'

TWENTY-FIVE

'She's still not answering her phone,' said Ray. 'It's not like her. I'm starting to get worried.'

'Chill,' said Wynnie. 'She's probably just dropped it somewhere. You know what she's like.'

His words hung in the air for a moment, and Ray tried to think it through. Nothing about this made sense. But nothing about anything in her life seemed to make sense now.

'Hey,' she heard Wynnie say. And then his hand was on her shoulder, warm even through her jacket. 'You OK?'

Ray wiped furiously at her eyes and sniffed. 'You must think I'm such a fool.'

'No, I don't. If you like we could go back, take another look.'

She blinked at him. 'Are you serious?'

'Truthfully? No.' Wynnie heaved a sigh. 'I haven't been so scared since Mr Daniels caught me hanging around the girls' hockey changing rooms in Year 9. But... if it'll make you feel better, we'll go back.'

'Really?'

'Really.' He grabbed her hand. 'Come on, let's go. We know what to expect this time.'

Ray stood up and looked closely at him. His eyes were so pale and so honest. She couldn't imagine him ever lying to anyone. 'Wynnie…'

He raised his eyebrows in that funny way of his.

'I just want you to know…'

They rose a little more.

'I… I'm… I'm *really* glad you're here with me.'

'That's good. Cos I'm really glad I'm here with you too.'

There was a pause and neither of them seemed to know what to say next.

'Come on,' said Wynnie eventually. Still holding her hand, he led her back towards the Black House.

TWENTY-SIX

'Harold?' said Ianto.

Jack helped the fallen man into a sitting position, but it was obvious that he was beyond help. Fresh green blood was running out of his mouth. Jack had produced a clean white handkerchief and jammed it against the bubbling wound in his chest, but the material was quickly soaked through.

'I'm sorry,' Jack whispered. 'I'm sorry, I didn't know—'

Harold licked his lips but only managed the faintest of croaks.

'I thought you were an assassin,' Jack insisted. 'We were expecting a gunman.'

Harold swallowed the blood in his throat and tried to speak again. 'Came… here… to help…'

Jack held him close. 'You said someone would come – a killer.'

'Not me, you fool.' Harold's eyes flickered and the vertical pupils narrowed to tiny slits in the amber irises.

'Check the Hub security sensors,' Jack instructed Ianto. 'We're still on red alert. If Harold teleported in then someone else could too. They might have already snuck in on his transmat signal.'

Ianto nodded and withdrew. Jack turned back to Harold, who was fading fast. His eyes fluttered closed and his breathing had become irregular and extremely shallow. Jack could feel the alien's cold green blood seeping through his own shirt.

'No chance… of survival…' Harold whispered.

'You'll be OK,' Jack insisted. 'We'll fix you up…'

'Under…taker's…Gift…' Harold's voice had dropped to nothing more than a breath – perhaps his last.

Startled, Jack pulled him closer, dipped his ear towards the blood-smeared lips. 'What? What do you know about the Undertaker's Gift?'

Long seconds passed while Harold summoned his last moments of life. 'Hokrala… don't understand… what they've set in motion…'

'What?' Jack demanded. 'What have they set in motion?'

'The end of everything… a world of suffering.' Harold coughed weakly, wetly, and a violent convulsion ran through his body. Jack tightened his grip as the alien's legs began to flail. His last seconds would see his nervous system overwhelmed with the pain of death.

But then the alien's hand suddenly grasped Jack's sleeve and pulled him closer, allowing him to breathe his final words:

'Already dead…'

'No you're not, Harold. Stay with me. We can get help…'

'Already dead… are here…'

All movement left Harold's body then, and he became nothing more than meat and bone. Jack lowered him gently to the floor and then sat back thoughtfully. He felt as if a vast, crushing weight had sudden come to rest on his shoulders.

'We're secure,' Ianto said, returning. 'I've reset the alarms.' He paused, seeing Jack bent over the body. 'Jack? Are you all right?'

'He's gone.' Jack climbed to his feet and took a deep breath.

Ianto pulled his gaze away from the corpse and looked at Jack. 'Were you close?'

'Not really. But I never wanted to *shoot* the guy.'

'That's really…' Ianto struggled for something to say and finished with '…bad luck.'

'Yeah, you could say that.' Jack frowned then, noticing something on the floor. It was a small plastic box about the size of a paperback book, lying near to Harold's outstretched hand.

Ianto picked it up, puzzled. 'It's a video cassette.'

'It's a message,' Jack realised. 'Harold brought it with him. He was trying to tell me something about the Undertaker's Gift.'

'But a video?' Ianto wasn't impressed. 'It's not even a DVD…'

'It's worse than that,' said Jack, taking the cassette. His shoulders slumped. 'It's a Betamax.'

TWENTY-SEVEN

At the Black House it was still eerily quiet, but there was no sign of the dark men.

'They've gone,' Ray said. She didn't know now whether to be relieved or disappointed. And, to her surprise, she realised that Wynnie was still holding her hand and a giddy rush of pleasure seeped through her whole body.

But then Wynnie let go of her hand to point towards the tree line. 'There's someone coming.'

For a second they almost panicked, until they realised it was just a woman – young, long black hair, rather striking in a leather motorcycle jacket and boots.

'Hi,' she said, without preamble or any kind of hesitation. She was clearly used to talking directly to complete strangers. 'Is this the Black House?'

'Uh, yeah,' said Wynnie.

'Who wants to know?' Ray asked. The woman was older and taller and more attractive than she was, and it suddenly felt important that she kept close to Wynnie.

'I'm Gwen Cooper,' the woman said. She smiled at them. 'You must be Rachel Banks and Meredydd-Wyn Morgan-Kelso.'

Both of them simply stood still and said nothing for a full five seconds. Ray felt a strange fear creep all over her, as if something had changed in her life that would alter things for ever, change things in ways that she couldn't even imagine. There was a sudden, dizzying feeling of everything being out of control now, of finding that she was little more than a leaf blown by the wind – at the mercy of forces she could never comprehend or withstand.

'Oh shit,' Wynnie said eventually. 'You're Torchwood, aren't you?'

Gwen Cooper just shrugged her shoulders. 'Is this where you saw the funeral procession?'

'Near here, yes,' nodded Wynnie. 'Apparently.'

Ray looked at him. '*Apparently?*'

'Well, I didn't see it. You did.'

'It was around here, yes,' Ray conceded. She spoke to Gwen. 'How did you know? I mean, I'm assuming you read my blog, but…'

'I told you not to mention Torchwood,' Wynnie hissed.

'We just want to find out what's going on,' Gwen told her. 'Like you.'

'I don't want to make anything official,' Ray said. 'I mean, I don't want to go to the police or anything. I could've done that, but I didn't. I don't want the authorities involved.'

'Of course not,' Gwen agreed. 'Anyway, we're not the authorities.'

'Aren't you a government department or something?' Wynnie asked.

'We deal with things that are too important to be left to the government or the police.'

Wynnie scratched his head. 'You're not going to wipe our memories, are you?'

'No,' said Gwen. 'Not yet, anyway.'

Wynnie smiled but Ray felt a flash of annoyance. 'I'm really

116

not bothered about Torchwood or whatever you are or with creepy funerals or anything. Right now, I just want to find my friend. She said she was going to meet us here and now she's missing and she won't answer her phone.'

'Gillian,' nodded Gwen.

Wynnie gaped. 'God, do you know *everything* about us?'

'Not everything, no.'

'Do you know where Gillian is?' Ray asked.

'No, but I might be able to help you find her. Try her mobile again.'

Ray looked immediately suspicious. 'What do you mean – again?' She bristled. 'Have you been listening in on my phone calls?'

'Do you want to find your friend or not?'

'We've already tried her phone,' Wynnie explained. 'She's not answering.'

Ray folded her arms. 'My mobile's gone dead anyway. Battery's done in.'

'Use mine,' Gwen said, tossing her own mobile over.

Ray caught it and dialled Gillian's number. A moment later they all heard a tinny, strangulated version of 'Kiss You Off' ringing out from somewhere nearby.

Ray and Wynnie both whirled around. 'Bloody hell! That's Gillian's phone!'

'It's around here somewhere,' Gwen confirmed.

Wynnie homed in on the ringtone just before the mobile cut over to voicemail. It was lying face down in a patch of scrubby, dead grass in the centre of the Black House. He picked it up and showed the display to Ray.

'Five missed calls from me,' Ray realised. 'And one unknown.' She looked down at Gwen's mobile in her hand and slowly closed it.

'She must've dropped it,' Wynnie said.

'No,' Ray disagreed. 'She wouldn't drop it – not Gillian. She might be a lot of things but she's careful with her phone because it's her life.'

Even as she said the words she regretted it. Because suddenly it seemed that the three of them were looking at all that remained of Gillian, lying in the palm of Wynnie's hand.

'She's been murdered,' Ray moaned. 'I know she has.'

'Perhaps,' Gwen said carefully, 'she dropped her mobile on purpose.'

'You mean like a clue?' wondered Wynnie. He looked sceptical. 'C'mon. That's way too cool for Gillian.'

Gwen was kicking at the dried grass and soil where the phone had been found. Wynnie realised what she was doing and joined in. They quickly cleared away a large patch of weeds and Gwen gave a shout.

'Here we go,' she said.

There was a large square shape cut into the stone. The crack that formed the perimeter was clear of dirt and free of grass, and the shape was unmistakable. A trapdoor of some kind. It had been opened recently and someone had tried to conceal it with a patch of dead vegetation.

'Might lead to a cellar or something.' Wynnie dropped to one knee and began to feel around for a handle. 'This was a church once, remember.'

'Churches don't often have cellars,' Gwen said thoughtfully. 'But they do have crypts.'

TWENTY-EIGHT

'There you go,' said Ianto, setting a large box down on Jack's desk. 'Told you it wouldn't be a problem. One Betamax video recorder, brand new, still in its box, top-loader. Fell through the Rift from 1982 in May 2008.'

'And you knew exactly where to find that?' Jack looked impressed.

'Cataloguing and storage. It's in my job description.'

'It is?'

'Everything in its place and a place for everything, as the actress said to the bishop.' Ianto fussed around, connecting a nest of wires from the VCR to one of the ancient black-and-white TV sets in the corner of Jack's office. He slid Harold's cassette into the large silver machine and they watched as the old Magpie TV warmed up, the screen slowly filling with interference before jerking into life as the video started to play.

Harold's sharp, white features filled the little screen and his voice crackled out of the speaker.

'Sorry about the use of such primitive technology, dear boy,' he said. 'The twenty-first century is so retro it's untrue. Hope I've got it right, anyway. If you're watching this then I'm probably already dead – I think there might be a couple of Hokrala heavies on my tail and I'm rather afraid they mean business.'

Jack and Ianto exchanged a guilty look.

'Time to cut to the chase,' Harold's 2D ghost continued. 'The Hokrala Corp use warp shunts to send stuff through to you and it's damaging the fabric of time and space around the Rift. That's how I've been able to flit back and forth and visit you like this. But it's also why there's such a lot of rubbish seeping through to the twenty-first century right now that you could probably do without.'

'That's true,' muttered Ianto.

'Hokrala are targeting your time period because they think it's a weak spot in Earth's history, and they're right.' Harold leaned in towards the camera, pointing emphatically. 'You're their Number One enemy, Jack. They've tried everything they can to get rid of you by legal means, but you've never been one to abide by the law. So they've sent some kind of assassin – I don't know who or what but I know they're already on Earth.'

Ianto and Jack looked at each other again. Jack eased the Webley out of its holster and Ianto reached for his automatic.

'Once you're safely out of the way, Hokrala can do whatever they want with twenty-first-century Earth,' Harold smiled thinly.

'Great,' said Jack. 'Tell us something we don't know.'

'But here's something you don't know,' Harold continued. 'Hokrala have found a way to activate something called the Undertaker's Gift. I've no idea what it is, apart from the fact that it is some kind of secret weapon and they've resurrected the last of the Already Dead to deliver it. That means bad news for Earth, Jack, whichever way you look at it.'

'The Already Dead?' repeated Ianto.

'Let me tell you about the Already Dead,' said Harold. 'They are suicide soldiers from the Keshkali Ring Worlds – their own solar system was destroyed by a temporal fusion device thought to have been concealed deep beneath the planetary crust by human hand. The resulting chronic spasm unravelled the molecular bonds of every living creature that was unfortunate enough to survive the blast. Those survivors have paid a terrible price for their continued existence. The Keshkali DNA has been devolved to a point where they can hardly exist in the physical sense at all, apart from the rags that hold their diseased remains together. They live in continual pain and they have a psychotic hatred of all humans. They've been made the guardians of the Undertaker's Gift and they're bringing it to Earth. They know they're doomed but they see this as a final chance for redemption. Where Keshkali went, they want Earth to follow.'

'A world of suffering…' Ianto said softly.

'You will have to fight them,' Harold said. 'The Already Dead is a state of mind for these chaps rather than a literal meaning, but that makes them no less difficult to deal with. They will be hard to take down – so if you intend to tackle them at any point in this time period with primitive projectile weapons then make sure you have enough firepower.'

'I think we'll cope,' Jack muttered.

'Sufficient impact wounds will overcome what the science boys calls the mutated lipid cohesion that holds them together. They'll literally fall apart. Which sounds like fun.'

Ianto raised an eyebrow.

'But they will be armed,' Harold continued. 'Compressed praxis gas flechette weapons. Don't underestimate them. One shot from those could pin a human being to a brick wall.'

'Which doesn't sound like fun,' murmured Ianto.

'Unfortunately that's all I can tell you, Jack,' Harold said. 'Except that the Already Dead are already here and you've got to stop them. The Undertaker's Gift is going to mean the end of everything unless you do.'

The TV picture shimmered and Harold looked nervously off camera at something Jack and Ianto couldn't see. Then he turned back to face his invisible audience and said, 'I think they're coming for me. I've got one chance to teleport and I'm going to try and get this message to you. If I don't make it… then good luck. Because you're going to need it, dear boy.'

The picture faded and the video clicked off in the machine. As it began to automatically rewind, Jack stood up and gazed out of the circular window which overlooked the rest of the Hub. Harold's crumpled corpse still lay where it had fallen.

'I'll tend to the body,' Ianto told Jack. 'There's no need for you—'

Jack shook his head. 'It's all right. We'll do it together. You look beat anyway.'

'What do you think about these assassins, then? If they were after Harold they might follow him here.'

'Let 'em come,' Jack growled. 'I'm in the mood for a fight.'

'I don't think they're planning on a boxing match. They're going to come armed and they're going to try and kill you.'

'Well, they're gonna be disappointed, aren't they? I mean, any kind of death threat is a bit pointless in my case. Either way, the Hokrala assassins are the *least* important consideration here.' Jack looked directly into Ianto's eyes, his own wide and blue and earnest. 'We have to start thinking about protecting Earth rather than me. If these goons turn up, we'll deal with them – we're ready. In the meantime we concentrate on the Undertaker's Gift.'

'All right,' Ianto nodded, blew out a deep breath. 'The Already Dead sound a lot like the people Rachel Banks and Francis Morgan's friend described. Maybe Gwen was right.'

'She usually is.' Jack smiled at the thought of her. 'Those police instincts will always lead her to the truth and she won't stop until she finds it. She's *our* secret weapon, Ianto.'

'And what am I?'

'Hot in a suit,' Jack said. 'As if you didn't know. C'mon.'

TWENTY-NINE

They stowed Harold's body in one of the freezer compartments in the Torchwood morgue. Jack watched stony-faced as Ianto pushed the drawer in and closed the hatch.

'We seem to have been surrounded by death recently,' Jack said thoughtfully. 'Everywhere we turn – corpses, graves, coffins, funerals…'

Ianto rested his head against the steel door and closed his eyes.

'Hey,' said Jack. 'You OK?'

'I don't feel too good, actually.'

'You don't look it. Take five, Ianto. Get your head down and rest. I'll tidy up here.'

Jack led him back towards the main part of the Hub. Ianto allowed himself to be steered to the low settee against one of the old walls, where he sat down heavily.

'Drink?' Jack asked. 'Coffee?'

Ianto looked up sharply, alarmed. 'No! I mean – no, thanks.'

Jack looked hurt.

'Making coffee,' Ianto explained patiently, 'is an art. Trust me on this.'

'How hard can it be?'

'No, Jack, really,' insisted Ianto. 'It would be like letting a chimpanzee loose with Van Gogh's paint box.'

'Gee, thanks.'

'No offence intended, but it is best left to the experts.' Ianto looked up earnestly and sighed. 'Sometimes, Jack, it's important to know your limitations.'

'I wasn't aware I had any.' A thought struck him. 'How about tea?'

Ianto shuddered. 'Water would be nice.'

'Comin' up!' Jack saluted smartly. 'You just hang on in there, Barista Boy.'

Ianto watched Jack move off and then sat back with a grimace. He wasn't just tired, he was in pain. There was a sore spot on his chest and he felt nauseous. He didn't want Jack to know how bad he felt because Torchwood was already understaffed. They couldn't afford sick leave, that was for sure – especially not now, during one of their busiest times ever.

Wincing, Ianto pulled his shirt up out of his waistband and felt his chest. He was sweating a lot.

He got up and went to the bathroom, where he took a good, long look at himself in the mirror. His skin was pasty and his eyes looked as if he had just been woken up from a deep sleep. He stuck out his tongue, which was grey and furred. He opened wide and said, 'Aaaahhh…' but couldn't see anything that looked especially wrong. Although he wasn't a doctor and wouldn't know what to look for anyway, he had once suffered a bout of septic tonsillitis and remembered the sight of the yellow ulcers at the back of his throat only too well. There was nothing like that now and, besides, he didn't have a sore throat.

Just a sore chest.

He opened his waistcoat and shirt and examined the skin. It looked normal enough, except for a dull red patch just below his ribs. It felt itchy but he didn't want to touch it. His mother had warned him never to scratch a rash in case it made it worse. There was some antiseptic ointment in one of the bathroom cupboards and he began to look for it.

'Ianto?' Jack's voice drifted in from the Hub. 'Water.'

'I'll be right out,' Ianto called back. 'Just give me a minute.'

He found the antiseptic cream and applied it sparingly to the affected area, following the instructions on the tube to the letter. His mother had warned him about that too. Owen, he recalled, used to open a bottle of medicine and throw the instructions away. 'Just a lot of crap about side effects written by lawyers,' he would say. 'You may experience the following symptoms: drowsiness, insomnia, dizziness, nausea, increased hunger, decreased hunger, loss of taste, loss of smell, problems with vision, with hearing, skin disorders, itching, stomach aches, headaches, hair growth or hair loss. Well, that covers just about everything so there's no point in trying to sue 'em. Ditch the small print and follow your instincts, that's what I always say.'

But Ianto was a small-print person. His life was based on precision. He put the ointment tube back in the box and closed the lid carefully. He returned it to its appointed place in the bathroom cabinet, alongside the other medicines, label outwards for easy identification. He would be able to find it in the event of a power-cut too, because he had arranged them all in alphabetical order.

He took some deep breaths and then splashed cold water on his face. He straightened up and dried himself off, swallowing bile. Then he fastened his shirt and waistcoat and fixed his tie. Ran a comb through his hair.

God, he felt awful.

THIRTY

'Maybe we should call the police,' said Wynnie nervously.

Gwen and Ray had managed to force open the hatch. At first Gwen had thought it might just be a drainage cover, long forgotten by the council and now a pointless adjunct to the remains of the Black House. But as soon as it creaked open she knew she was onto something. She felt the familiar pulse of excitement in her chest and stomach as a narrow flight of stairs was revealed leading down into the darkness.

Leaves fluttered past, the sky darkening, ready for a storm. Gwen took a deep breath and made her decision. To hell with Jack – she'd do this herself and show him there was no need to hold her hand all the time. She reached into her jacket pocket and produced a small but powerful LED torch.

Without waiting – fearful that she might change her mind if she thought about it too much – Gwen started down the steps, stooping as she went below ground level. The torchlight wavered in front of her. 'Are you coming or staying?' she called over her shoulder.

'Staying,' said Wynnie, and at the same time Ray said, 'Coming.'

Ray looked sorrowfully at Wynnie. 'I've got to go. I want to find Gillian.'

'That's a job for the police,' Wynnie insisted.

'But Gillian's barely been missing for an hour or so – the police won't do anything about that. She's an adult. They wouldn't do anything until she'd been gone a day or more. OK, so we found her phone – but what does that prove? Nothing. She dropped it.'

'Everything about this,' said Wynnie carefully, 'is bad. Wrong. The whole place feels… wrong.'

'Exactly. And how do we tell the police about that? Or about the pallbearers from the funeral cortège?' She reached out and rubbed his arm. 'Come on, Wynnie. Let's check this out ourselves first, while we can. We've come this far.'

He drew a long breath. 'If you're sure…'

She almost laughed. 'I'm not sure about *anything* any more.'

'All right,' he said heavily, taking her by the hand. 'Let's do it.'

They went down the steps, hurrying after the torchlight. At the bottom of the stone steps was a narrow, brick-walled passageway. It was noticeably colder and damp down here.

'How do you two feel about rats?' asked Gwen as they caught up.

'Um,' said Ray, in the manner of someone who wanted to say, 'I can't stand the bloody things.'

'There are a few down here,' Gwen explained. She was trying to sound unconcerned and, to her credit, almost managing it. 'They're steering clear of the light, though.'

She shone the torch down the passageway and a number of grey shapes darted away into the shadows. 'Yuck.'

'Actually, I quite like rats,' said Wynnie. 'I used to have one as a pet.'

'Good for you,' said Ray. She pulled him closer. 'I had cats. Work it out.'

'It widens out a bit here,' reported Gwen. She had moved

ahead, and her voice echoed dully from the walls. In the torchlight they could see streaks of green where the damp had really got a hold and allowed things to grow.

'Smells funny down here,' Wynnie said. 'Like an old toilet.'

'Just watch your step,' Gwen warned. 'It's a bit uneven and wet underfoot. And then it looks like there are more steps ahead.'

'Going down?'

'Yup.'

'I might have guessed,' Wynnie grumbled. 'Are you sure this is the right thing to do?'

'You can go back if you want,' Gwen told him.

'He's staying with us,' Ray said. 'Aren't you?'

'Looks like it.'

They went carefully down the next flight of steps. These were not as steep as those that led down from the surface, but they went on for longer. It was very cold and damp. A crowd of rats suddenly dispersed as Gwen's torchlight found them. Their shrill cries disappeared into the gloom along with their lank, grey tails.

'Not enjoying this any more,' said Wynnie plaintively.

'Shh.'

'What are we listening for?' whispered Ray.

Gwen held up a hand for silence, waited for a few heartbeats, then said, 'Dunno. Thought I heard something. Probably just the rats.'

She started forward again, and Ray made sure she and Wynnie stayed close. 'So, you do this all the time, do you?' Ray asked. 'I mean, for a living?'

'Sort of,' Gwen said.

'You know, I've been thinking,' Wynnie said. 'And I've decided that I really, definitely, completely do not like this one little bit.'

'Honestly,' said Ray. 'You're like Shaggy in *Scooby-Doo*. What's the matter with you? Get a grip.'

'I'm beginning to understand how Shaggy felt,' Wynnie said.

'But at least he had Scooby to back him up.'

'Hold it.' Gwen stopped, shining the torch at her feet. 'Recognise that?'

There was a little handbag lying in the circle of light: blue suede with a white dog on it.

Ray swallowed, feeling sick, a hand to her mouth. 'That's Gillian's bag. Oh my god, that's her bag.'

Wynnie gripped her arm. 'Steady. It doesn't mean she's down here. Thieves could've stolen it, dumped it down here when they'd finished with it. Kids, even.'

'He's got a point,' Gwen said, kneeling down. She used a pen to tease the handbag open a little and shone her torch inside. 'But it looks like the purse and all her stuff are still in here. I can see a couple of loose pound coins too. So probably not thieves.'

'OK.' Wynnie swallowed hard. It was probably his imagination, his natural fear of the unknown, but some nameless dread was forming a tight, uncomfortable knot in his chest. 'I *really* think we should all go back now,' he said.

'But Gillian could still be down here,' Ray insisted.

'Just a few more minutes,' Gwen promised.

Wynnie looked unsure. 'All right. I'll stay too. But only because of you.'

Ray smiled back at him and squeezed his hand. 'It's OK,' she told him. 'We'll be fine.'

Gwen had ventured further ahead. 'It looks like this might lead to some sort of crypt. There's a doorway here.'

In the torchlight it looked very dark, but then something moved in the shadows beyond and a figure stepped into view. Gwen, Ray and Wynnie all jumped and the torch beam jerked wildly before settling on a pallid, round face surrounded by matted blonde hair.

'Gillian!' gasped Ray, stepping forward. 'Oh my God!'

Gillian stared back at her without saying a word, clearly in shock. Her eyes were wide and frightened and she was shaking.

'What happened to you?' Ray wondered. 'I thought you were dead!' She held out a hand. 'Come on, let's get you out of here. Wynnie's here with me and this is Gwen…'

But then Gillian opened her mouth. Something glistened inside and a dark liquid began to ooze down her chin as if she was dribbling ink.

Ray recoiled as Gillian lurched stiffly towards her. Her mouth began to work as if trying to say something, but the effort seemed immense.

'Go…' The word was coughed up with more black slime. 'Go… and never come back…'

The words slipped from her lips on a dark river of unguent and then she tumbled forward, crashing to her knees on the concrete floor. She fell forward onto her face without making any effort to break her fall, the impact echoing down the passageway with a sickening crunch.

Ray was staggering backwards, her eyes wide, the breath tearing from her chest in panicky gusts. Gillian lay on the floor, quivering as a pool of blackness opened up beneath her.

Dimly, Ray was aware of Gwen pulling a large, blocky gun from the waistband of her jeans and pointing it along the passageway. There were more figures coming through the door now – tall, dark men with faces swathed in old, stained bandages.

The pallbearers.

In the fitful light of Gwen's torch, their eyes glittered between the tiny slits in the bindings.

'Go!' Gwen shouted, jerking her head back along the corridor. 'Run!'

Ray felt her hand grabbed by Wynnie, and together they began to stumble backwards, nothing in their minds now except a blind desire to put as much distance as possible between themselves and this awful, underground world.

But Wynnie ground to a halt before they had even begun to run.

'There's more,' he said in a fearful whisper. 'We're trapped.'

There were more pallbearers standing in the passageway behind them. Slowly they began to walk forward, gloved hands outstretched.

THIRTY-ONE

'Keep back!' Gwen yelled, levelling the Glock. If she squeezed the trigger now, it would send a tungsten-cored 9mm parabellum bullet straight through the centre of the nearest pallbearer's bandaged forehead.

Gwen never opened fire unless it was absolutely necessary – but she had to establish some kind of control of the situation here, and urgently.

'Hold it right there,' she ordered. She summoned every ounce of conviction she could muster, trying to sound confident and assertive. She made sure that the barrel of her gun did not waver at all. She held it up at eye level and gazed unblinkingly along the sight, lining up the luminous foresight with the V notch at the rear of the pistol.

'One more step,' she said forcefully, 'and I'll put a bullet in you. That's a promise.'

She gripped the automatic tightly, trying to ignore the fact that her hands were sweating.

The pallbearer took absolutely no notice. It moved forward, stepping over Gillian's body, continuing in its unhurried path towards Gwen.

She squeezed the trigger and watched as a third eye opened up in the pallbearer's forehead. The sound of the shot – a deep, shattering boom that reverberated deafeningly in the confines of the tunnel – seemed to follow a half-second later, preceding the dark stain which spread through the surrounding bandages.

But the pallbearer continued to walk towards her, hands outstretched.

Gwen's lips tightened and, aware of the desperate wail of Ray behind her, she fired again. And again. Shot after shot struck the figure in the head, neck and chest as she tried to smash every vital organ she could find. Blackness oozed from the ragged, smoking holes and, gradually, the pallbearer seemed to falter. Gwen stood her ground, made sure her aim stayed true, and put another bullet right in the centre of the bandaged face. Suddenly the creature's whole head seemed to cave in, the filthy wrappings sagging as the figure pitched forwards, finally collapsing in an inert heap.

But there were others behind it, and Gwen's pistol was more than half empty. She finished off the mag with no attempt to take careful aim and then turned, grabbing Ray with one hand to propel her forwards.

'There's more of them behind us!' moaned Wynnie as the dark shapes filled the passageway.

'We've no choice!' Gwen shouted. 'Go! Run!'

She shoved them both forward, hooking a fresh magazine from her jacket pocket and slapping it into the butt of her gun. She cocked it and opened fire again, pumping bullets rapidly into the oncoming figures. They jerked and recoiled and spewed dark, treacly blood but it was clear they weren't going down easily.

The nearest pallbearer reached out for Gwen and she swung her Glock as hard as she could into its face, letting it crunch right into the bandages. Gloved hands scrabbled for her, grabbed her hair and yanked hard. With a shriek, Gwen found her head wrenched backwards, her body twisting to follow. Her feet kicked out as the pallbearer dragged her backwards, tightening its grip in her hair, pulling her into its cold embrace. Her heart pounded madly and panic flooded through her veins. Fragmented thoughts flickered through her mind – she was losing her grasp on the gun; Rhys would never find her; she should have told Jack before coming down here; she was going to die...

And then, as if from a great distance and over the rasps of her fearful breathing, she heard Wynnie's shout:

'They've got Gwen!'

And then suddenly he came barrelling back down the passageway, screaming like a madman, arms flailing. And somehow he struck lucky – his fist smashed away the pallbearer's hand and the grip on Gwen's hair vanished. The pain was enormous – it felt as though half her scalp had been torn out – but she hardly registered it because she was suddenly, impossibly, gloriously free.

Ray seized her hand and pulled her upright and together they half-ran, half-fell away from the tumble of bodies. Until they heard a hoarse yell of fear from behind them and turned to see Wynnie's terrified face lost in the midst of all the confusion.

His eyes locked onto Gwen's and he gasped, 'Run!'

Gwen grabbed him with her free hand, beating at the pallbearers with the butt of her gun. Wynnie had come back to save her and now she would do the same for him. But the pallbearers had a much better grip on him and Wynnie seemed to be paralysed with fear. His eyes were wide, wild, and his mouth was hanging open in a terrified, silent rictus.

For a moment Gwen found herself locked in a bizarre tug of war. Wynnie's hands clenched around her wrists as she tried to pull him free, but the pallbearers were insanely strong.

'Help me!' The words sprang from Wynnie's lips in sudden, urgent grunts, as if this is all that his brain could come up with. 'Help me! Help me!'

'Pull!' screamed Gwen. She could see the malevolent glare of yellow eyes between the bandages of the pallbearers behind Wynnie, she could see the deadly intent to compete with her for the life of the boy. Ray joined her, her hand scrabbling for a grip on Wynnie's arms and together they pulled him back, shoulders scraping against the brick walls, feet sliding on the muck and filth that lined the floor.

The pallbearers, suddenly losing ground, increased the savagery of their efforts. Gwen could see their fingers curling like steel talons into the thin flesh of Wynnie's shoulders and she felt, rather than heard, the dull scrape of bone on bone. Wynnie's mouth widened as a groan of pain and despair filled the tunnel. His eyes whirled in their sockets, searching for Ray.

'Ray!' he heaved the word into the air, just before a gush of black vomit filled his throat and ran over his lips.

'Wynnie!' screamed Ray.

Gwen watched in horrified fascination as the dark emetic surged from Wynnie's nose, darkened his eyes and trickled down his face. It was almost as if the murky filth that filled the pallbearers' bodies had somehow infiltrated Wynnie, filled him with a torrent of evil and then overflowed.

He suddenly went loose in her grip and she felt him slipping. Ray was screaming, and her fingers fell away from the boy's sleeves at the same time as he suddenly reared, shaking as if gripped in the jaws of a giant, invisible dog. The veins beneath his skin had darkened as the alien matter surged through them, forcing them to stand out like a road map on his face. Then he was discarded, thrown with deadly force against the wall where his skull burst like a rotten fruit and disgorged a lump of sticky, tar-like brain.

It had only taken seconds, but something, somehow, had changed his entire physical composition.

Ray staggered backwards, away from the carnage, her mind racing wildly, trying to make sense of what she had just witnessed and at the same time looking for a way to escape. There was a sudden lull, almost silence, as if each side was pausing to take stock of the situation. The pallbearers stood over Wynnie's shattered remains, facing Gwen, while Ray backed rapidly away.

'What have you done?' asked Gwen thickly. There was anger as well as fear in her words now. 'What did you do to him?'

The pallbearers made no reply. They stared implacably at Gwen from the shadows and then slowly moved forward, stepping over Wynnie's corpse. Towards her.

She raised the automatic again. 'Keep away,' she said, but there was an unmistakable tremor in her voice now. She could barely stand.

She only got one shot off. As she pulled the trigger and sent another bullet somewhere into the mêlée, lost among the dark figures, the leading figure suddenly moved like lightning. Almost as if events had been speeded up, just for two seconds, the pallbearer closed in on Gwen, wrenched the pistol from her fingers and reached for her face with its other hand.

THIRTY-TWO

Ray ran like she had never run before.

All that concerned her was escape. There had been a momentary gap in the ranks of the pallbearers, a dark space for her to dart through and bolt. It was enough.

The walls of the passages sped past her in a blur. She couldn't see clearly because it was so dark and the tears were pouring from her eyes, and she was running blind, feeling her way along the dank tunnels, and in seemingly no time at all she had reached the steps that led up to the next level. She surged up them, lungs bursting, certain that there would be more of the pallbearers coming up behind. She reached the next landing, pounded through the mud and leaves and found the base of the steep steps that led up to the dim square of light that was the outside world.

Suddenly her legs were as heavy as lead. Those last few steps to freedom felt impossibly hard. There would be clawing hands reaching for her, grabbing at her clothes and legs, if she didn't hurry. Ray laboured up the steps, wheezing, broke out into the cold, cold light and fell heavily to the floor.

Silence.

After a moment, Ray started breathing again, long, ragged, sobbing breaths.

She was out.

But she wasn't free.

She would never be free – she knew that. Because even as she lay there panting, retching, clawing at the blessed ground with her fingernails, she knew that Wynnie was gone. For ever.

The memory came back to her in tiny little spurts – all that she could bear. Momentary, flickering images in her head – Wynnie's anguished face, the black liquid gushing from his mouth. The distended veins, creeping over his face like some horrible tattoo.

And mixed in with all this were the lingering, rain-cold flashbacks to the funeral cortège the night before: the pallbearers, the casket, the indescribable contents.

Suddenly, Ray jerked herself upright. She couldn't allow herself to think like this. Lives were at stake. She had suddenly remembered Gwen – she had been convinced the Torchwood woman was bringing up the rear, chasing her for the exit, but there was no sign of her.

She crawled back to the hole in the ground. Peered cautiously over the edge, down into the darkness.

But there was nothing.

No one.

Not a sound.

Ray wanted to shout Gwen's name, to see if there would be any response, but she was frightened of attracting unwanted attention. She didn't want to see the pallbearers again. Ever.

She sat back and looked around the deserted church.

There was no one here. No one to call to, no one to help. No one to understand.

She was completely alone.

She stood up, in a daze. There was still no sound from the hatchway, not an echo or a rustle or anything.

138

Just a deadly silence.

And she knew then, beyond all doubt, that Gwen was lost. The pallbearers had taken her.

Numbly she wondered what to do. She stood, enclosed in the thick silence, just her and the black hole in the ground at her feet.

THIRTY-THREE

Jack helped Ianto into the Autopsy Room, which was full of every kind of medical equipment.

Ianto sank heavily onto a step. 'What's wrong me with me, Jack?'

'I don't know. But I intend to find out.'

'You're not a doctor,' Ianto pointed out with a weak smile.

Jack raised an eyebrow, affronted. 'I told you I don't have any limitations.'

'Or qualifications for that matter.'

'Qualifications! Who needs 'em?' Jack started to check through the medical stores, picking up bottles of medicine and putting them back again. 'I mean – white coat, stethoscope… how hard can it be?'

At that moment Jack's phone rang. He whisked it from his pocket and checked the display, a look on his face that mixed anticipation with relief in roughly equal parts.

'It's Gwen,' he said, answering the call. 'Hiya, what you got for me?'

Ianto saw the minute but clear change that overcame Jack's face as it happened: a sudden, slight stiffening of the jaw, a fractional narrowing of the eyes, the warm, clear-sky blue replaced in an instant by an arctic chill. A furrow appeared in the normally clear brow.

'Who is this?'

Ianto watched, puzzled, now ignoring the growing sense of nausea that continued to sap his strength. There was a tinny voice answering Jack, who had himself gone suddenly pale.

'Who are you?' Jack demanded again. 'Where's Gwen Cooper?'

He thumbed the loudspeaker button on the mobile so that Ianto could hear the reply. A young, female voice stammered through the silence of the Hub:

'I – I don't know… She's gone… They've both gone…'

Ianto started to say something, but Jack silenced him with a sharp gesture.

The girl's voice continued: 'Wh-who is this?'

'I'm Captain Jack Harkness.' Another change came over him now: he took a deep breath, straightened his shoulders, and somehow let all the tension ease away from his face. His tone grew softer, warmer, but still carried an unmistakable authority. 'You're through to Torchwood. Now why don't you take a minute and then tell me your name?'

Despite the calm, engaging words, Ianto noticed that's Jack's knuckles were still ivory white where he was gripping the phone.

'R-Ray. My name is Ray…'

'Hi there, Ray. Cute name for a girl. What's happened?'

'I – I don't know… one minute we were all together, we were in the Black House… and the next it all kicked off with the pallbearers, they were there, waiting for us and they killed Gillian and then they killed Wynnie as well and oh my god *oh my god* they're dead what am I going to do—'

'Whoa, whoa. Slow down. Take a deep breath. Go on. It's OK, Ray, you can tell me all about it – but you gotta tell me one thing at a time.' Jack raised his eyebrows at Ianto. 'You said the Black House?'

'Yeah, I'm there now.' Ray's voice was childlike, agonisingly brittle. 'I think you'd better call the police or something.'

'Just tell me what happened. I want to know where Gwen Cooper is. You're using her phone.'

'She… gave it to me. To ring Gillian, before we found the door. I – I must've put it in my pocket. I didn't think. Please, you've got to help me.'

'Where are you now, Ray?'

'I'm still here. At the Black House.'

Jack looked at Ianto, signalling to him that he should get the SUV ready. Ianto turned and headed for the cogwheel door, Jack following as he talked to the girl. 'Tell me what happened to Gwen.'

'It's not just her. Wynnie's dead too.'

Jack's mouth turned dust dry. He followed Ianto along the access tunnel that led to the SUV garage, his thoughts flying wild. After a second he composed himself, summoned his patience, licked his lips. 'Just tell me what happened, Ray, as best you can.'

'The pallbearers got them. I don't know who they are, but they did something to Wynnie and it was horrible. Awful. He's dead and it's my fault. I made him come with me. He didn't want to go inside, but I made him.'

'Stay calm. I can only help you if I have all the facts.' Ianto opened up the SUV and Jack climbed into the driver's seat. 'What about Gwen?'

'She's dead too. They got her as well. And Gillian too. Oh god, this is *terrible*—'

Jack's fingers were hurting where they gripping the mobile hard enough to crack the plastic. 'OK, Ray,' he said, carefully and calmly. There was no indication of stress in his voice at all. He hit the SUV starter and the powerful, zero-carbon engine rumbled into life. He eased the steering wheel around one-handed as he gave the mobile to Ianto to hold. The SUV turned towards the exit ramp and picked up speed. 'Listen to me. You say you're still at the Black House, right? Great. We're coming to meet you, Ray. We can be there in less than fifteen minutes – let's make it ten. Do you think you can wait that long?'

'I – I don't know…'

'Tell me you can, Ray, because it's important.'

'All right. I th-think so.'

'Good girl. Find somewhere safe and hang tight. Keep hold of that phone.'

'OK. OK.' The voice sounded small and frightened, even through the loudspeaker. Shock was beginning to set in, the words sounding numb and emotionless. 'I'll wait here. Who did you say you were?'

'Captain Jack Harkness.' The SUV roared out of the underground garage into the cold, evening light and surged onto the road. 'And this is Torchwood.'

THIRTY-FOUR

The cold hands pulled Gwen down until the darkness took her.

Perhaps this was what dying was like: Jack had once described it as a cold, infinite darkness. Or perhaps, she guessed in a spasm of panic, it was the poisonous black gore of the pallbearers infiltrating her body and killing her slowly and painfully from the inside out. Like Wynnie.

But then she felt herself dropping through the grasp of the hands to hit the floor, hard. She closed her eyes and lay there, unmoving, not even daring to breathe. If she could have stopped the pounding of her heart she would have done so.

The pallbearers moved around her, above her, the ragged hems of their long coats brushing her face and hair as they passed. She kept still, dead in every visible manner, her cheek pressed to the filth of the concrete floor.

Wynnie was dead, and there was no sign of Ray. It crossed her mind that the pallbearers could have left her to pursue the student – and they would surely kill her when they found her. Gwen fought down the dull ache of despair in her stomach. She had to make those deaths mean something. She had to live and find a way to fight back.

Whether it was Torchwood training, or instinct, or the fact that Gwen had faced death many times before, she didn't know. But she wasn't dead yet and that always had to count for something.

She waited for a minute longer until she was satisfied that she was alone. It was during this period that Gwen became aware of the pain in her left ankle. As soon as she moved the pain grew worse. It must have been sprained – perhaps even broken – in the fight with the pallbearers. But she couldn't just lie here and do nothing. She had to move. Gritting her teeth, Gwen started to crawl laboriously along the passageway.

She could hear someone breathing – long, hard, painful gasps, so loud that they must have come from someone very close. She froze. The breathing stopped. And only then did she realise that it was her own breathing she could hear.

Come on, Gwen, she told herself. *Get a grip.*

She clenched her fists and crawled on. The floor of the tunnel was covered in a cold sludge but she knew she had to ignore it. She had to get to the exit, get out in the open and warn Jack and Ianto. She didn't have her mobile any more – she vaguely remembered that Ray had kept hold of it – but there was no signal this far underground, and her earpiece wouldn't work for the same reason.

She had to get out, however difficult and painful it was.

Then she heard movement further down the passageway. There was definitely something there, a dark presence in the shadows. She stopped and glared at the gloomy shape, her eyes wide. For a split second she hoped that it was Ray, that the girl had somehow survived. But she knew in her heart that was impossible and, besides, the figure she could see was too tall.

It was a pallbearer, standing guard near the exit. It stood like the shadow of a statue, no indication that it was even alive or breathing. And there was no reason why it should be, at least by human standards. Gwen felt a little flutter of excitement in her stomach, the same world-changing thrill she always felt when in the presence of something alien to Earth. No matter what the danger, the buzz was always there.

There had been times when she had enjoyed the kick that danger brought: the sheer, unadulterated joy of facing death or injury and surviving it. That sensation could become addictive. She had never seen herself as a thrill-seeker, but she could understand the attraction. Facing down death, beating it, was better than sex. Not that she would ever tell Rhys that, but it did go some way to explain why Captain Jack Harkness was so incredibly *hot*.

You're losing it, Gwen told herself angrily. *Your mind's starting to wander.* The adrenalin high was giving way to delirium, and the pain in her foot was starting to add a persistent, bass-line beat to everything she thought. If she analysed the feeling properly, she knew that she would suddenly begin to appreciate just how brain-numbingly painful her ankle was. She had to take her mind off it somehow.

There was no way to get to the exit, not with the pallbearer there, that much was clear. She had to go the other way, maybe find somewhere to hide.

Very slowly, very quietly, she turned herself around. She bit her lip hard as the pain in her ankle flared with every movement, but eventually she was facing in the opposite direction and she was able to crawl away from the exit, and deeper into the shadows.

She had no idea where all the pallbearers had gone; they had simply disappeared into the passages and tunnels like rats. At last, Gwen was able to sit up and take stock of her position. She was filthy, exhausted, injured and in need of a really big vodka.

She edged further into the blackness, shivering. It was damp and unforgiving down here and she was close to panic. She had to keep calm, use her training, remember that the only way to meet a crisis was with a cool head.

A little further down the passageway she found Wynnie and Gillian.

The pallbearers had moved them. They had taken the bodies and pinned them to the walls of the passageway, opposite each other, like a pair of gargoyles. Metal spikes, slightly flared at the ends like darts, had been driven through their arms and legs to hold them to the brickwork, and two more had been driven through the eye sockets of each of them to pin back their heads. Congealed, tarry blood ran from the shattered eyes down the grey cheeks, staining the clothes like ink.

Gwen resisted the urge to vomit. She had been at road traffic accidents where the carnage had been unbelievable and kept control of her stomach; she had seen death before in many and varied forms during her time with Torchwood. And she had always kept the sick down. She refused to give in. The sight was ugly and distressing, but the physical violence didn't affect her as much as the realisation that this abominable act had been carried out with cold deliberation by the alien beings who had come here, to her planet, uninvited.

The bodies were a warning: *Come any further and the same thing will happen to you.*

But Gwen Cooper didn't back down to bullies. Never had, never would. This kind of thing didn't frighten her, it just made her more determined than ever to put a stop to it, to do her bit to protect the human race from this kind of hostile action.

Because what Gwen saw here was nothing short of a declaration of war. Whoever, or whatever, the pallbearers were – wherever they came from and whatever they wanted – they had just bought themselves a whole load of trouble.

With a choking sob, Gwen lowered her eyes, ground her fists into the grime beneath her, and crawled onwards, further into the darkness.

THIRTY-FIVE

Ray sat on the remains of a low stone wall at the edge of the Black House.

Shock had set in after she had disconnected the call to Torchwood. The American man had sounded nice – warm, confident, in control. But it felt like a dream now. The moment she had closed the call and the mobile's backlight had faded, the whole conversation had felt like a ridiculous flight of fantasy.

Torchwood? Captain Jack *Whatever*…?

It was ridiculous, and she would have felt ashamed if it hadn't been for the calamitous avalanche of shock and despair that had descended on her since escaping from the crypt with her life.

With her life.

Wynnie was dead. She couldn't comprehend that simple, incontrovertible fact. She knew it was the truth, but she just couldn't *comprehend* it. Couldn't feel it. All she knew was that a huge, boiling rock of fear and grief had landed on her chest. And it was suffocating her.

Ray had no idea how long she sat like that; time no longer had any meaning at all. A river of bad thoughts swirled through her mind, slow and murky with guilt.

She had survived. Her friends were dead. And she had absolutely no idea what to do now.

Then she heard the car engine. A big, black 4x4 slewed to a halt directly in front of her, the tyres scrunching heavily across the cracked paving.

Two men got out of the car. The first wore a serious expression and a three-piece suit. The second man was older, good-looking and wearing an RAF greatcoat. He strode purposefully towards Ray and she saw that he had a pair of the most wonderful blue eyes she had ever seen. As he approached Ray she automatically got to her feet, and a slow smile softened the man's otherwise diamond-hard glare.

'Ray?'

'Yes.'

He held out his hand. 'Captain Jack Harkness.'

His hand was as warm and dry as his voice. Ray found herself shaking the hand automatically, and a curious sense of calm seemed to rise up her arm and spread through her entire body. Just being near him was like being wrapped in warm towels. She staggered slightly, her legs almost giving way as the accumulated emotional turmoil suddenly dissipated.

'Easy now,' said Jack, keeping hold of her hand, supporting her. The briefest flash of a smile sent a wave of renewed strength and energy flooding through her.

'This is Ianto Jones,' Jack told her, nodding at the man in the suit. 'We're Torchwood.'

Ray looked back at the SUV. 'Just the two of you?'

They didn't reply. The man called Ianto had some sort of handheld device which he was using to scan the area.

'What happened to Gwen?' Jack asked.

'She went down there with Wynnie and me,' Ray said. 'We were looking for my friend Gillian. She said she was going to meet us here.' Ray quickly recounted the facts about finding Gillian's mobile, the underground passages, the pallbearers. She spoke in a flat, dull voice, unwilling to let her emotions surface now. She barely wanted to think about it at all, but she knew this was a job that had to be done. Her voice gave up on her, however, when she started to recount the details of Wynnie's death.

'What happened to Gwen?' Jack repeated.

He was making an effort to be patient, Ray could sense it. There was a small muscle in his jaw that she could see was twitching. She took a deep breath and tried to explain, but all that came out was a jumble of senseless words.

'OK,' he said, holding up a hand for her to fall quiet. 'Let me ask you this question: did you see Gwen Cooper die?'

Ray was about to start nodding, because she was certain that she *had* seen Gwen die at the hands of the pallbearers – but then, in a sudden moment of terrible clarity, she realised that all she had seen was… nothing. She hadn't stopped to check. She had turned and fled. And as she had run helter-skelter along the darkened passages, Ray had thought Gwen had been running right behind her. But she hadn't followed Ray out of the Black House so she must have been mistaken. Gwen must have been killed along with Wynnie and Gillian.

That was the only possible explanation. But she hadn't actually seen it happen, and she said so. 'No. No, I didn't.'

Jack Harkness nodded to himself with just a hint of relief and satisfaction, and then turned to Ianto Jones. 'Anything?'

'Low-level Rift activity,' Ianto reported, still checking the PDA. 'Faint signs of antilositic energy traces. Nothing conclusive.'

'Shielded?'

Ianto shook his head. 'No sign of anything like that.'

Jack turned slowly on his heel, letting his gaze take in their surroundings: the scrubby weeds, broken walls and leafless trees. The empty shell of the church. He shivered, visibly, as he returned his attention to Ray. 'Can you feel it?' he asked.

'What?'

'The weight of the future,' Jack replied. 'Pressing down on us.'

He closed his eyes and breathed in deeply. 'You can feel it in the air. Like the universe is holding its breath.'

'Do you really know what's going on here?' Ray's voice sounded small, lost.

'Not really. But I've lived in these parts for long enough to sense when something is wrong, and round here... it's really wrong. Badly wrong.'

'Can you put it right?'

'We can try.' Jack turned to Ianto. 'We need to go down and take a look.'

Ianto nodded in curt agreement, switched off the PDA and turned back towards the SUV.

Ray watched him go and then turned back to Jack. 'Are you mad? You can't go down there. I told you – it's full of those pallbearer people. They'll kill you.'

'No chance,' Jack replied.

'But there's only the two of you.'

'Don't worry,' Jack said. 'We've brought some friends with us to help out.'

Ianto returned with a heavy canvas hold-all, a bit like a cricket bag. It looked heavy, and when he dumped it on the ground it made a harsh, metallic clank. Ianto unzipped the bag and Jack picked out a short, brutal-looking sub-machine gun.

Ray stepped back, amazed and somewhat aghast.

'Meet my old pal the Sten gun,' Jack said. He snapped a long magazine into the side of the stock and cocked the weapon with a loud, aggressive action.

'This is insane,' said Ray.

'This is Torchwood,' Jack replied.

THIRTY-SIX

Gwen couldn't work out how deep she was under the Black House now, or how far she had come. The twisting maze of dark passages was now just a confusing, nightmare memory. She had crawled until she couldn't stand the pain in her ankle any longer, and now sat against a cold, wet wall. Her jeans were soaked through, her jacket was torn and filthy, and she was starting to shake.

She felt in her jacket pocket and found a spare magazine for her gun. But she had dropped the automatic somewhere in the initial fight so the ammo was next to useless. In her other pocket she found her pencil torch. She took it out and, after a few seconds work with her trembling fingers, managed to switch it on. She kept one hand cupped over the end so that the small but powerful LED didn't suddenly illuminate the whole area and give away her position.

Very carefully, she allowed a small, thin ray of light to seep out between her fingers. It stabbed through the darkness, caught the mud-streaked toe of her left boot. Her foot was throbbing now, sending bolts of pain right up her leg and deep into her chest.

She angled the torch beam so that it cut across the passageway, finding the opposite wall in a coin-sized spot of light. It was green, wet, shrouded by old cobwebs. She roved the light across the uneven brickwork until it disappeared into a black abyss.

A doorway, right opposite her.

Cautiously, she probed the floor with the torch. It looked like quite a wide door. Tracing the edge of it upwards, she discovered a low, arched stone ceiling stained with wide, irregular patches of moist lichen. It looked like the map of an alien world, scrawled in decay across a dark, forgotten heaven.

The old church crypt.

Wonderful.

Gwen slowly pulled herself around and crawled on her hands and knees through the doorway. Every now and again she had heard the distant sound of the pallbearers moving around in the passageways and she guessed they were still searching for her. She hoped that they were too arrogant to realise that the corpses of Wynnie and Gillian hadn't been enough to scare her off.

She raised the pencil torch and directed it into the darkest shadow. The light fell on a smooth wall of glass, smeared with greasy marks and streaks of algae. It was some kind of tank, or container, long and low.

Like a funeral casket.

The light found its way through a clear section of the glass. At first, there was nothing to be seen but the darkness beyond. The casket appeared empty.

But then something moved inside it. Slowly, calmly, with a soft, dry rustle. An indistinct shape moved into the light of Gwen's torch and she saw then what it was.

She didn't scream. She couldn't. The noise simply died in her throat, strangled by fear.

THIRTY-SEVEN

The Sten gun was clutched tightly in Jack's hand as he reached the bottom the first flight of steps leading down into the Black House crypts. His eyes peered sharply into the darkness, but the place was deserted.

'Quiet as the grave,' remarked Ianto, joining him. The cold evening light seeped down the stairs after him, casting a wan grey light across his features. It didn't make him look any better.

'How are you bearing up?' Jack asked him softly.

'I've felt better,' Ianto admitted. He was carrying a Heckler & Koch MP5 SMG and it looked heavy in his hands. The strap bit into the bone of his shoulder and the flesh of his neck was as white as his shirt collar.

'I can't do this alone,' Jack told him quietly. 'Just hang in there and cover my back, OK?'

'OK.'

Jack moved forward and was swallowed up by the shadows in an instant. Sweating profusely, Ianto started after him.

When they couldn't see any more, they switched on their torches. Ianto's was clipped to the barrel of his MP5. Jack carried his in one hand, the Sten gun in the other.

'Are we expecting a lot of these characters then?' Ianto wondered.

Jack kept his reply to a whisper. 'I don't know. But you remember what Harold said. The Already Dead are suicide soldiers. They won't spare us and we can't spare them. They're hard to kill but not impossible – we'll just have to hit them with everything we've got.'

They continued along the narrow passageway and descended the next flight of steps. Jack's boots squelched through the mud that lined the tunnel floor, his torchlight searching for the next level. Then, for a fleeting moment, the light struck a piece of ragged cloth that suddenly vanished, its owner recoiling from the glare with a sharp hiss.

Jack paused, crouching, shining his torch along the passage. Suddenly something grey lurched out of the darkness, a humanoid in a long, ragged cloak. The Sten gun let out a deafening rattle and the figure crashed backwards with an angry snarl.

Jack leapt down the rest of the stairs as the creature rolled to its feet. In the light of Ianto's own torch, he could see the front of the alien's chest, swaddled in bandages, filthy with blood. The creature's head snapped up, the black mouth yawning open between the layers of bandages.

And then the nightmarish face caved in under a deafening fusillade of bullets from Ianto's H&K. One moment there were the bandages, with tiny yellow eyes glittering with hatred, and the next there was just a sticky black mess, and the figure collapsed backwards.

There was another directly behind it, stepping into the light with a hiss. Jack, already on one knee, opened up again with the Sten. Tar-like blood jetted from the ragged holes in the creature's chest and neck and it, too, fell. The creature writhed on the floor, its ragged hands clutching at the brickwork on either side of the passageway. Jack stepped over the kicking heels, put the Sten to his shoulder and aimed another burst directly into the head. The body gave a final jerk and then lay still.

The clattering echo of the automatic gunfire was still reverberating down the passageway.

'Well, they know we're here now,' Ianto said, breathing hard.

'Damn right,' said Jack. His face was grim as he knelt down to examine the corpse. Carefully, he hooked a finger under some of the bandages which covered the face and pulled them free, shining his torch on what was revealed beneath. He winced at the sight, and quickly turned the light away. 'The Already Dead,' he said. 'Worse than I thought.'

'If I didn't feel ill before, then I do now,' said Ianto weakly.

'Poor creature,' whispered Jack. 'What kind of life could a thing like this lead? A rotting, humanoid effigy, held together by filthy bandages. Doomed to an existence of pain and suffering.'

'So we're putting them out of their misery?'

'Maybe.' Jack stood up slowly. 'They'll really be coming for us now, though, Ianto. And they'll have nothing to lose.'

Ianto leant against the wall and took a couple of deep breaths. The sweat was running down his face now. 'You realise that Gwen is probably dead.'

'I know.' Jack's lips had compressed into a thin line. 'But until I see her with my own eyes, Ianto, I won't accept it. And if I have to fight my way through an army of these pallbearer guys to do it, I will. Are you with me?'

'All the way.'

There was a noise like a cough from the darkness and something metallic clanged against the stonework by Ianto's head. He ducked, and another steel bolt ricocheted away into the shadows. Jack swung his torch around, illuminating a pallbearer at the far end of the passage holding a long spear. It was pointed directly at him. With a sharp grunt of compressed gas, the flechette at its tip was suddenly launched towards Jack's face.

THIRTY-EIGHT

It was spread across the crypt like a giant spider's web, a complex network of wires and tubes radiating from the central casket and disappearing into the darkness.

At the centre was a container of some kind, shaped like a coffin but more like a fish tank. The glass was murky and stained with green algae, as if whatever was kept inside had been organic and rotten.

But since that time, the container had been expanded, reconstructed, to accommodate what lay within.

The creature inside was clearly dead. The movement she had seen earlier had been nothing more than the reflection of her torchlight in the dimmed glass. At first, all she saw was the body – a withered, grey ribcage mottled with dark sores. The blood was so old it had turned into a black crust surrounding the damaged areas. The head, little more than a bulbous skull, was covered by skin so shrunken to the bone that what remained of the lips was pulled right back from two rows of uneven, grey teeth. The nose had gone, eaten away by parasites, leaving a ragged hole beneath the eye sockets, where creased, long-dead lids were fused shut over sunken eyes.

So far, just another corpse – ancient, dried up matter, the leathery effigy of an unknown man.

But someone, or something, had been working on this corpse. Both the head and torso were held in place by a series of metal rods and pins, skewering the body and bolted into place. The metal was dull and rusted, and the flesh was fused to the pins wherever they entered.

There were no arms or legs. The trunk tailed off to an abdomen which consisted of shrivelled organs hanging like stuffing from the rags of torn skin. The lower part of the spine was visible at the base, trailing off to a series of broken, age-browned vertebrae that just managed to glint with a touch of ivory in the light of Gwen's torch. Leading into the desiccated remains of the intestine were old rubber tubes, like the kind found trailing from gas taps in laboratories, cracked and perished and snaking away to a series of bottles and stands beneath the casket. There were some wires, too, thick with insulation, but in places Gwen could see that the copper wiring had come adrift where the flesh had dried and withdrawn.

She stared at the mess, frowning, trying to work out what could possibly have happened but failing. It looked like it was all that was left of some kind of dreadful Victorian experiment, and it made her shudder with revulsion.

But not as much as what had been done to the head.

The top of the skull had been cut away and removed, like the top of a boiled egg. Stealing herself, Gwen aimed the light into the cranium, where a dried-up brain, like a giant walnut, rested in a web of rotten flesh. Wires had been fed into the brain matter, inserted through the folds in its surface. They emerged from the skull like a fright wig, leading up and away into the shadows. Some were as thick as mains flex; others were thin, but grouped together and tangled like spaghetti.

Troubled, revolted, frightened – but unable to stop searching for some reason or clue as to who or what had done all this and why – Gwen narrowed her gaze. She directed the torchlight into the skull, inspecting the grizzled contents. She felt her stomach turn as she became aware of tiny things moving in the flesh, little white grubs slowly feeding on the old meat, their bodies pulsing with life in the sudden, harsh light of her torch. She felt herself starting to retch and pulled back, turning the light away, returning them to the privacy of their midnight feast.

Gwen took a moment to gather her wits. What had happened here? Who had done this? Why were the pallbearers protecting this ancient, abominated corpse? The questions whirled around in her head, but there were no answers.

Something clicked in the casket.

Steeling herself, Gwen pointed her torch at the skull. It remained unmoving, unflinching. Dead, except for the maggots at work inside. Gwen watched in revulsion as a millipede emerged from the dry cave of the mouth. It ran down the chin like a stray morsel of food and disappeared into the thin, stringy remains of the neck.

She'd seen enough. It was time to leave. Whatever the pallbearers were doing in the catacombs behind her, it had to be better to take her chances with them rather than stay a second longer in the company of this foul, forgotten experiment.

'Heh…'

It was little more than a gasp, a breath, a single word half-formed in the shrivelled remains of its throat. But Gwen knew it had spoken because she saw the exposed Adam's apple move and a puff of dust escape through the holes in its neck. The teeth parted slightly as the jaw trembled in its attempt to work.

'Hello…?' it repeated in a slow, dry wheeze. 'Who is it? Who's there?'

The mouth cracked open a little wider, disgorging shreds of a blackened tongue and more millipedes.

'I know you're there!' it said. *'I know you're there!'*

THIRTY-NINE

The flechette glittered in the torch beam and Jack, with lightning reflexes, batted it away. It clattered loudly against a wall, showering him with brick dust.

He aimed the Sten one-handed and sent a burst of machine-gun fire in the direction of the pallbearer. There was nothing but shadow at the far end of the tunnel now, and the bullets kicked up a storm of chipped stone and metal in the blackness.

'This way,' Ianto said, pulling Jack away.

The passage branched left and right a little further on. There was not a sound to be heard anywhere, and nothing to see in the darkness. Rats hurried past their feet, but they ignored them.

'No more sentries?' Jack wondered quietly. 'That can't be right.'

'I know. It feels like we're being watched.'

They shone their torches down the passage but there was nothing to be seen. The light played along the rough walls, picking out bits of weed growing thinly between the cracks, and lumps of damp moss speckling the brickwork.

Something reached down from above, two skeletal arms swathed in rags. Long, curled fingers clamped around Ianto's shoulders and he gasped in pain, automatically lifting his torch to shine it upwards. The light found the hissing, spitting face of one of the pallbearers, hanging from the ceiling. Others were crawling along behind it, like giant, ragged spiders, their long claws gripping the brickwork upside down.

Jack whirled, opened fire, spraying the creature and the ceiling beyond it. The pallbearer released its grip on Ianto with a breathless squeal and withdrew, clawing its way swiftly back towards the shadows with the others, but Jack kept his finger on the trigger, firing along the ceiling. Splinters of bricks and mortar filled the passageway but eventually the bullets found their home in the back of the retreating pallbearer, shredding the material of his cloak and thudding through the flesh beneath. It hissed furiously and disappeared into the darkness beyond the reach of his torchlight.

The Sten magazine had clicked on empty. Jack hurled it away and snapped another into place, cocking the weapon in one smooth, easy motion.

'You've done this kind of thing before,' remarked Ianto.

'Helped clear the Nazis out of Berlin at the end of the war,' Jack explained. 'I fell in with a platoon of Commandos. We had to clear some parts of the city house by house. The Nazis were hiding like rats, and when they were cornered they fought. Although they didn't crawl along the ceilings.'

He started along the left-hand passage, the way the pallbearers had come. He kept the flashlight roving ahead, including up the walls and ceiling.

Ianto waited a second or two, trying to get his breathing and heart rate under control. He could feel the thud of blood in his ears, sense the rash on his chest burning. But Jack needed him so he had to push on. He swallowed back the hot reflux that kept bubbling up his gullet and pushed away from the wall. Tightening his grip on the MP5, he staggered after Jack.

FORTY

'What was that?' the voice rasped. The skull jerked a little as the wiry, shrunken tendons in its neck tried to move. 'I thought I heard something…'

Gwen stared, wide-eyed, at the head. Just a head, with a body. No arms, legs, and a tangle of wires and tubes rising from its exposed brain and guts. Impossible, obscene.

Alive.

'It sounds like gunfire,' Gwen heard herself saying. Her voice sounded small and scared.

'Speak up!' ordered the corpse. 'I can't hear you!'

Gwen seriously didn't know whether to scream or laugh now. This was both horrific and ridiculous at the same time. She just didn't feel capable of entering into a conversation with a corpse. And yet…

'You're… alive?'

'What was that? I told you to speak up!'

'How can you be alive?' Gwen asked. There was a tremor in her voice, but she was determined to ask the question. 'I mean, how *can* you…?'

'Did you say gunfire?'

'Yes, yes I did. It sounded like that to me. There must be something going on in the crypt…' Gwen shook her head, ran a hand through her hair. A part of her thought the gunfire meant that help had arrived, possibly even Jack and Ianto. But she couldn't afford to hope, and neither could she afford to let this opportunity slip by.

Gwen took a tentative step forward. She had inspected the body in great detail originally, but now that she knew it was still alive she felt intrusive getting too close. The thing was clearly blind, and there were still insects crawling in and out of the body, but somehow she felt that this wasn't just a rotten cadaver.

It was a person.

'Who are you?' she asked, speaking a little more loudly this time.

'Frank,' said the corpse. 'Who are you?'

'My name… is Gwen.'

'Are you new here? I don't recognise your voice. I can't see a damned thing any more.'

Gwen opened her mouth to reply but then closed it again.

'I don't like it here,' said Frank. 'They don't look after you properly. And the nurses never speak to me.'

'Nurses?'

'You'd think they'd look after me better,' Frank continued. 'Considering.'

'Considering…?'

'What I went through – what we all went through. War is hell, love. War is *hell*.'

'Wait a second,' Gwen suddenly made the connection, like a light flickering on inside her head. 'Are you *Francis Morgan*?'

'Yes.'

Gwen blinked. 'You were injured in the First World War.'

'First? What are you talking about?'

'That was over ninety years ago…'

'I know I've been here ages, love, but it's not *that* long…' A

163

low chuckle escaped the dried lips. 'Though you can lose track of time when you can't see any more.' He started to cough, a pathetic, wheezing hack that produced nothing but dust and insects. 'Say... you couldn't get me a glass of water, could you, love? I'm parched.'

FORTY-ONE

The passageway split again. Jack and Ianto covered both with their guns, but the mouths of the tunnels yawned back at them in dark contempt.

'Which way now?' wondered Jack.

They stood still for a few seconds, straining to listen.

'I can't hear anything,' Ianto said.

He slung his MP5 and checked the readout on his PDA. The screen lit his face up bright blue in the darkness.

'There's more chronon activity that way,' he said, nodding left. 'And that antilositic energy trace is getting stronger too. That's got to be it.'

Jack looked at him, saw the dark circles under his eyes in the light of the PDA. 'You OK to carry on?'

'Of course.' Ianto was leaning against the wall, his breathing shallow. 'Just needed a moment to get my breath back, that's all.'

'Easy,' said Jack, as Ianto's eyes rolled up into his head and he slumped down the wall. Jack caught him, lowered him as gently as he could.

'Got a rash,' murmured Ianto. 'It hurts, Jack.'

Jack licked his lips. 'Ianto, I need you. It's not over yet. You gotta get up.'

'Give me a minute.'

Jack thought for a second and then, quickly as he could, he unfastened the buttons on Ianto's waistcoat.

'You pick your moments,' Ianto said.

'Hush. I'm checking something.' Jack lifted Ianto's shirt and examined his chest in the light of his torch. A look of surprise, and then revulsion, crossed his features. Both were quickly replaced by a look of cold anger.

'What is it?' Ianto asked. 'What's wrong?'

'Never you mind.' Jack quickly tucked the shirt back down and forced a smile. He patted Ianto on the leg. 'We'll deal with it later. Right now I need you on your feet.' He hooked an arm under Ianto's shoulder and pulled him upright.

Ianto groaned. 'It hurts.'

'No pain, no gain.'

'How much further?'

'I don't know. But I really need your help, buddy. Those creeps will be back any second, and I'm not leaving until we find Gwen.'

Ianto nodded and gripped his MP5. 'OK.'

Jack nodded once and they continued down the left-hand passage. Here the darkness was cold and complete, swallowing the light from his torch in one easy gulp. Suddenly a stark, ragged figure lunged out of the shadows and he opened fire with a yell of surprise. The bullets threw the pallbearer backwards, blood spraying briefly in the torchlight before the creature disappeared into the gloom.

Another took its place, and Jack dropped to one knee, firing again. The pallbearer staggered forward, absorbing the hail of gunshots, reaching out for Jack with clawed hands. The fingers scrabbled against the barrel of the Sten, but another burst of fire chopped the hands into lumps of torn meat and bone and the creature screeched in pain.

The Sten's magazine had emptied. Jack smashed the metal butt into the pallbearer's face, catching the bandages and ripping them open. Insane yellow eyes flared in a face of congealed black slime, until a barrage of fire from Ianto's MP5 turned the head into paste. The pallbearer slumped on top of its mate, but there were more behind it.

Jack was changing magazines when he heard – dimly, because his ears were still ringing from the close-quarter shooting in such a confined place – Ianto cry out. Twisting around he saw a pair of bandaged hands gripping Ianto by the throat. There was a pallbearer behind him, on top of him, trying to break his neck. The curled fingers dug deep into the white flesh of Ianto's neck and his face was creased in pain.

Jack hurled his fist past Ianto's own head and straight into the face of the pallbearer, connecting with a wet crunch. The pallbearer shuddered, and Jack punched it again, harder this time, squaring his shoulders for maximum follow-through. The fingers loosened their grip just enough for Ianto to fall free, gasping and choking.

Jack used the Sten as a club once more, jabbing the stock into the face and neck of the creature until it hissed and tried to swipe it aside. Its hands were scrabbling for Jack's throat as he turned the Sten back around and tried to pull the trigger, but he hadn't been able to cock the mechanism and it didn't fire. For a second or two Jack and the pallbearer were locked together, Jack searching with his free hand for a grip on the thing's face. His fingers found the eyes and dug in hard, slime bubbling out from between the bandages. It let out a harsh, silent squeal and backed off.

'Pincer movement,' Jack gasped. 'They've caught us in a goddamn pincer movement!'

'They're getting smart,' Ianto warned.

'We're gonna be surrounded—'

'Look out!' growled Ianto, shooting back the way they had been facing. Another pallbearer fell into the darkness, stung by the MP5.

Jack's own pallbearer was coming back, dark tears staining its face. The bandages parted to reveal a wide, gaping slit of a mouth. Jack pulled his Webley from its holster and put three bullets through the mouth and out the back of its head in a cloud of blood and torn material. It collapsed as the booming roar of the pistol echoed down the passage like thunder in the night.

FORTY-TWO

'That's gunfire all right,' said Francis Morgan. 'I'd recognise it anywhere.'

'And I'd recognise the sound of that revolver anywhere,' Gwen said, a sudden wave of relief flooding through her. 'It's Jack!'

She limped painfully back to the doorway and called down the passage: 'Jack! Down here! It's Gwen! This way!'

Her voice echoed madly and she heard an answering volley of what sounded like an SMG.

She turned to Frank. 'I think someone's coming to rescue us,' she said excitedly. 'I mean me. I mean—'

'It's a bit late for me, love,' said Frank. His voice rasped in the still air. 'There's nothing for any of us invalids now. We're the leftovers of the war. Blind, legless... what is there for me now?'

Gwen didn't know what to say. 'I'm sorry,' she ventured at last. 'I'm really... sorry.'

'I wish I could see you,' said the rotting skull. 'You've got a kind voice. I bet you're a real smasher.'

Gwen felt her throat constrict and the tears welling up in her eyes. She stepped closer to where Frank's limbless torso dangled in its nest of metal spokes and wires and tubes. His head, held secure by thin metal bolts, looked parchment-thin and so delicate, as if a single touch would cause it to crumble.

'You have no idea, do you?' she asked gently. 'No idea of what the situation is down here.'

'It's bloody awful, that's what it is,' the skull insisted. 'If I get out of here I'm going to complain.'

'Do you remember how you came to be here?'

'They came and took me from the military hospital in Calais. That's where I woke up after the bomb blast. They said it was a 1,000 pounder. Left a hole fifty feet deep.'

'Do you remember who took you?'

'Not really. Lost my sight in that blast. Couldn't hear much for a long time afterwards, either. And to tell you the truth my hearing's pretty poor now. The bombs do that to you.'

'Yeah,' agreed Gwen faintly.

'They didn't say much when they brought me here. I haven't heard from any of my mates, even though I keep asking. They just operate on me, I think, when I'm strong enough. Must be a big job though. I remember a pal of mine who got his jaw shot off in Ypres.' Frank pronounced it 'Wipers', like all the Tommies in their day. He seemed lost in recollection now. 'Took seven operations and a piece of his thigh bone screwed into his face before he could even talk again. And even then no one could understand a word he bloody well said. I hope I'm not *that* bad.'

The tears were streaming down Gwen's face now, leaving white tracks in the grime.

'Do I look all right?' Frank asked in a plaintive tone. 'I mean, be honest, love. I know I was never much to look at, but will I scare the missus when she sees me?'

Gwen stared at the decimated skull, the hole where the nose had been and the sunken eye sockets. The brain matter inside the head was still crawling with worms.

'No,' Gwen whispered hoarsely. 'You look fine, Frank.'

Something made a noise in the doorway behind her and Gwen

swung around, flashing the torch. A pallbearer stood framed in the entrance, its bandaged visage half hidden beneath a hood. Slowly it raised its flechette weapon and aimed it at her head.

FORTY-THREE

Gwen stared dumbly at the pallbearer, just before it was thrown aside by a hail of automatic gunfire. Smoke rolled into the room and through it strode Captain Jack Harkness, clutching an old-fashioned sub-machine gun.

The light from his torch found Gwen's face and he rushed forward, throwing the Sten gun aside so that he could embrace her. He whirled her around with a loud whoop of joy. 'Thank God you're alive!'

'How did you get here?'

'Rachel Banks told us.'

'She got out?'

'Just. We thought you were dead, Gwen.' Jack held her close, kissed her, looked deep into her eyes. 'She told us you were dead,' he whispered hoarsely.

'Well I'm not. I've got a busted ankle but otherwise I'm OK. Where's—'

Ianto followed Jack into the room, sweeping his torch around until the light fell on the monstrosity in the centre. He levelled his gun.

'Stop!' Gwen shouted. 'Don't shoot!'

Ianto hesitated for a moment, his aim already wavering. He barely looked strong enough to hold the rifle up to his shoulder, and had to lean against the doorway. 'What is it?' he asked roughly.

'It's – he's Frank Morgan,' said Gwen. 'He's… still alive.'

Jack moved cautiously forward, taking in the tubes and wires and the limbless cadaver. He stopped in front of the ravaged skull and swallowed hard. After a pause he smiled and said, 'Hi, Frank. How ya doing?'

The skull twitched. 'You a yank?'

'Sort of.'

'What's yer name?'

'Captain Jack Harkness.'

'Officer, eh? Pardon me if I don't salute, mate.' The paper-thin lips cracked into a ghoulish smile. 'I knew a yank once. He was with us at Ypres. Name of Hank Schengler. We called him Hank the Yank. He was a good bloke.'

'That's nice. What are you doing here, Frank?'

'Good bloody question. I'm supposed to be convalescing. Got myself blown up and shipped back to Blighty. They've been moving me from hospital to hospital ever since and now they've brought me here.'

'You're not in hospital, Frank.'

Gwen touched Jack's arm. 'Jack, don't…' she said quietly. 'He doesn't know…'

'What d'you mean, I'm not in hospital? Where am I? What is this?'

'It's bit difficult to explain.'

'It's all right. I think I can guess. This is where people like me come to die, isn't it?'

'Actually, it's a bit more complicated than that.'

There was a pneumatic hiss of a flechette weapon and a metal spike embedded itself in Jack's shoulder, spinning him around. Jack let out a yell of surprise and pain and collapsed to one knee, his fingers scrabbling at the bolt.

Gwen whirled round to see the pallbearer standing in the doorway. Ianto was standing right next to him, already bringing his assault rifle up. The pallbearer hadn't seen him, and the barrel of the gun was practically touching the side of its head when Ianto pulled the trigger. The pallbearer's skull disappeared in a black mist of blood and shredded bandages and the bullets went on to carve chunks out of the wall opposite.

Ianto sagged backwards, the rifle dropping as what meagre strength remained finally left his arms. But as the decapitated pallbearer sank to the floor, two more appeared behind it, spears levelled.

Gwen rushed at the first, grabbing hold of the end of the weapon and heaving it sideways. The pallbearer, taken by surprise, allowed the stick to be dragged from its grasp. Gwen, screaming as her ankle gave way again underneath her, swept the handle of the stick upwards to connect with the creature's jaw, hurling it backwards.

The second pallbearer stepped past its falling comrade, weapon extended. It released its blade with a deadly hiss, and the flechette clattered into the ground where Jack Harkness had lain a second earlier. He rolled, came up on one knee, aimed the Webley carefully and put a heavy .38 calibre slug right through the creature's brains – or whatever it kept inside its head.

'They're trying to get in,' Gwen gasped, sinking to the floor and clutching her ankle.

'No kidding,' Jack said. For a minute there was silence, save for the painful echoing of the gunshot. Smoke drifted across the bodies piled in the doorway. Jack crossed over to where Ianto sat against the wall. 'You OK?'

He nodded, smiling weakly. 'You've got another hole in your coat.'

Jack reached up and pulled the flechette out of his shoulder with a grunt of pain. Blood glistened in the ragged tear of his greatcoat. 'You're gonna be busy with that needle and thread.'

'Jack, I don't feel well.'

A look of anguish crossed Jack's face. 'Hang in there, Ianto. We've come this far. We're not gonna stop now, right? Soon as we're done, I'll get you to a doctor.' He forced a smile to his lips and winked. 'A proper doctor.'

But the smile faded as something cold and metallic touched the side of Jack's head.

'Jack…' whispered Gwen.

'I got it.' Jack didn't need to look round to know that the razor-sharp tip of a pallbearer stick was now resting against his temple. Any second now the blade would slam into his skull and skewer his brain. He kept very still.

Two more pallbearers stepped past him and crossed over to the hideous contraption in the centre of the room. Frank Morgan had fallen strangely silent.

'OK,' said Jack softly. 'You've got us. What's happening?'

The flechette tip probed a little deeper, slicing the skin. Jack felt a trickle of hot blood run down his face.

'Y'know, you guys really need to loosen up,' Jack said. 'Strong and silent is one thing. Downright rude is another. I asked you a question: what's going on?'

The pallbearers, flanking the corpse in its glass casket, turned to face the doorway without another word. Another of the Already Dead followed them in, forcing a small, frightened figure in front of it.

'Ray,' said Gwen, surprised.

FORTY-FOUR

'I'm sorry,' Ray said. Her voice sounded choked with fear. 'They came after me. Just like I said they would.'

The pallbearer marched Ray across the chamber to stand next to the casket. Ray cringed as she saw the contents and tears flooded down her face. Confronted by the nightmare vision she had first seen the night before, Ray found herself unable to think or speak. But that didn't matter any more, because something was about to do the thinking and speaking for her.

The pallbearer grabbed her by the back of the neck, digging its long, grimy fingernails deep into her flesh. She gagged, eyes bulging in their sockets and the pain hit home. She hunched her shoulders up, trying to dislodge the grip, but it felt as if a tourniquet had been applied to her neck. She couldn't move. She was completely paralysed.

She could see Gwen looking up at her, her face a mask of anxiety and tear-streaked mascara.

Ianto leant against the wall, pale, eyes hooded, waiting.

Captain Jack stood between them both, one hand clutching the bloody mess of his shoulder. His eyes never left Ray's. 'Let her go,' he said firmly.

And then it happened. Ray let out a sharp gasp, purely involuntary, as a cold, unyielding pain slammed into her. It felt as if a thousand nails had been hammered simultaneously into every inch of her skin.

She fought against the grip of the pallbearer but it was useless. The strength was draining out of her with every passing second, replaced by a horrible, dreading numbness. She felt as if something cruel and alien was flooding through her veins, turning her blood into a thick, cold jelly. Bile rose in her throat, making her retch, and she felt a chill slime running down her chin. Panic filled her then, and her vision darkened as if her tears had turned to oil. And it was at that moment that Ray realised the truth.

She was about to die, just like Wynnie.

And that was her last natural thought. Because then she became aware of something else inside her – a presence, a person, something alien and wrong and nothing to do with her, invading her mind and body. Thoughts that were not her own started to wriggle inside her head, looking for a way out. Her tongue writhed in her mouth as if it didn't belong there and she heard a voice speaking – her own voice.

'Human filth!' She spat the words across the room, as if they had taken form as the dark, sticky matter in her mouth. 'Prepare for the end.'

'What have you done to Ray?' Jack's voice sounded a long, long way off.

'We use this animal to speak to you.' Ray said the words but they were not her own. She was a puppet, and she felt overwhelmed with an inescapable, burning sense of abuse and shame.

Jack spoke again. 'Who are you?'

'We are the Already Dead. We are here to bring about the end of your world.'

'Why? What for?'

'No explanation is needed. The time has come for this planet to die.'

'Now just hang on one minute.' Dimly, Ray could see Jack stepping forward, hand out, imploring. His eyes were wide and focused entirely on her own. And she could guess what he would see: her face, grey and taut, black tears running down her cheeks, lips smeared with dark, alien bile. She could feel her heart heaving in her chest, straining against the inhuman sludge that now filled her veins and arteries.

'Listen to me.' Jack took another step closer, carefully, slowly. He spoke softly. 'I've got to understand. What's going on? Why are you doing this?'

Ray's voice ground out its reply: 'There is no explanation necessary.'

'There must be! Why else would you take that girl and use her like this? You want to communicate? Go ahead, I'm listening.'

'This planet is fractured. The fault line runs through all four dimensions.'

'They mean the Rift,' realised Gwen.

'We've got it under control,' said Jack. 'Torchwood has a Rift manipulator—'

'A toy.' The pallbearer's thoughts forced their way out through Ray's lips. 'You have no understanding of the power of a Time Rift. How could you? Your civilisation has arisen in the blink of an eye, and thinks it understands the universe. Such arrogance. Such temerity. You look up to the stars and see wonder and beauty when you should see terror and ugliness. There is nothing but death and pestilence waiting for you and yet still you live in hope rather than fear.' Ray felt the black spittle fly from her lips as she spoke the pallbearer's words. 'If you knew anything about the universe, you would run back screaming to your primordial slime and never return.'

'Someone got out of the wrong side of the bed this morning,' Ianto muttered.

'You can't destroy us,' Jack said, although his words sounded hollow. 'You mustn't—'

'Enough. It is time for the end. We knew that the Time Rift was too important, too dangerous, to be left in the charge of mere humans – stripling minds, weak and blind as worms in a cosmos more complicated than you could ever imagine. We installed a failsafe here – a device that could be used if and when the Time Rift fell into enemy hands. That time has come.'

'Enemy hands?'

'Your hands.'

'We're not your enemy.'

'Nevertheless, you cannot be allowed to govern this Time Rift.'

'You've got us all wrong,' said Jack. He was trying to keep his voice calm and authoritative. 'We don't seek to govern. We try to… regulate. Control. It's damage limitation.'

'There is no limit to the damage a Time Rift can cause. And this one is too dangerous to be left to the likes of you. The device will be deployed.'

'What do you mean,' asked Gwen carefully, 'by *device*, exactly?'

'When the Time Rift was opened, the plan would automatically come into operation. A suicide unit would be despatched to Earth to set up a temporal fusion device that would use the power of the Rift to eradicate the human race. The planet will be cleansed by opening a controlled time fissure.'

'No one has ever opened the Rift,' said Jack carefully. 'Well, not recently.'

'Hokrala,' said Ianto. He stepped closer to Jack. 'The Hokrala Corporation has been backwards and forwards through time, using the Rift. That's what Harold told us.'

'Warp-shunt technology,' Jack recalled. 'They've been forcing the Rift wider with every trip. Allowing things to come through with them. *They* set all this in motion… they caused this insane plan to be put into operation – and they didn't even realise it.' He looked at the pallbearer. 'This isn't our fault. We haven't opened the Rift. Like I said, we monitor it, clear it, keep Earth safe…'

'The situation cannot be allowed to continue,' the pallbearer stated. Ray's voice had grown more ragged with every sentence. Now it was little more than a bubbling croak. 'We have come. The device has been activated.'

'What device?' Jack repeated.

'There is no device,' Ianto said. He held up his PDA scanner. 'There is no technological equipment here *anywhere*. I've checked and double-checked.'

'The device does not rely on technology as you know it,' Ray answered. 'Our systems were designed long before life evolved on this planet. You would not – cannot – understand.'

'It's Frank,' said Gwen, with mounting horror. 'You've used him, haven't you? All this…' she gestured angrily at the tubes and wires that stretched from the casket into the dark corners of the room. 'This is your device, isn't it?'

'The device is all around us.'

Gwen aimed her torch upwards, at the ceiling. The light beam trailed the wires and tubes which led from Frank Morgan's casket into the darkness, and then rippled across a surface full of strange, twisted shapes. The tubes sank into orifices all over the ceiling, which had a disturbingly organic texture. Ianto was aiming his own torch at the walls, which were similarly full of weird lumps and branches. At first it looked as though some tree roots had thrust out of the crypt walls, but then it became obvious that this assumption was wrong.

'Oh my God,' breathed Gwen. A tear ran down her cheek and her lips trembled as she realised what she was seeing. 'Please tell me it isn't true…'

The roots ended in angular, withered claws – the shrunken remains of skeletal hands. And the rest of the mass surrounding it resolved under careful scrutiny, like a macabre optical illusion, into the decaying bodies of animals and people: Weevils, dogs, cats, rats, human beings, all squashed together into one twisted mass, flesh fused together as the putrefaction had broken down the tissue over the years.

'Antilositic energy,' Ianto realised. He rechecked his PDA, the blue light flickering across his anguished face. 'Why didn't I realise? It was there staring at us all along. No need for electronics or mechanics. It's living tissue. They've used living tissue.'

'This man is the control element of the device,' said the pallbearer, and Ray felt her hand jerk towards the casket at the centre. 'He will undertake the final activation.'

'Undertake?' echoed Ianto.

And then it hit Jack like a hammer blow. 'The Undertaker,' he said softly. 'Frank Morgan.'

'And this is his gift to you,' said the pallbearer. With that, it released its grip on Ray.

The last thing she felt was a sudden coldness as if she had been immersed in ice water.

Then nothing.

FORTY-FIVE

Ray's blackened corpse collapsed at the feet of the pallbearer.

'No!' screamed Gwen, and in that instant Jack had whipped his revolver up for a snap shot, his finger yanking on the trigger in his haste to slay the pallbearer.

The shot went wide, the bullet scything past the side of the pallbearer's head.

It missed because Jack had rushed his shot, possibly the final, most vital shot of his long life. And he had rushed it because the pallbearer had brought up its own weapon at the very same instant and fired at him. Jack saw the flechette glint in the torchlight, and it filled his vision in less than a second, aimed straight at his forehead. But he was already moving, flinching away, using reflexes that were born of a lifetime of dodging death – and sometimes failing.

The blade glanced off the side of his skull and embedded itself in the wall.

Jack spun, the Webley flying from his hand. He crashed to the floor at Gwen's feet, where she knelt to help him up. The skin at the side of his head had been sliced open to the bone, in a long gash stretching from his right eyebrow to the back of his ear. He lay still, his eyelids fluttering.

'Jack…!' Gwen turned his face towards her, felt the hot blood running over her fingers.

A shadow fell over them.

She looked up and saw the pallbearer. Its narrow yellow eyes blazed down at her from between the bandages.

And then a deafening crash of gunfire sent the pallbearer hurtling backwards, flipped practically head over heels in a spray of black slime. It rolled to a stop next to the casket and melted slowly into the flagstones.

Ianto sat clutching the MP5, smoke curling up from the barrel. His finger was still clenched on the trigger, the magazine emptied. His face was a mask of white fury.

The other pallbearers were all sinking slowly to the ground, their mission complete. They expired with soft, liquid noises, oozing away through the cracks between the flagstones. They left nothing but piles of bandages and rags and a stench of death.

'We've got to… stop it…' Ianto croaked. 'The Undertaker… got to stop it…'

Gwen looked back at the casket. Frank Morgan's emaciated skull was twitching and jerking and pulses of luminescence were shooting out along the plastic tubes connected to the rest of the chamber.

'What's going on?' Frank's voice broke through the strange, heavy silence that had filled the crypt like glue. 'Am I back in the trenches? All I can hear is shouting and gunfire. Tell me I'm not back on the front line… Lord, but I don't want to die…'

His voice fell away to a thin whine. The tubes were beginning to glow now, flickering like fluorescent lights as the pallbearers' unnatural device came online. The crypt was lit by an ethereal green light, and Gwen could see the tubes throbbing and pulsing like living things, see the alien juices flowing inside like blood through veins. As the light grew brighter she could see the dead things that lined the walls starting to move as well, ancient tendons and dried muscles twitching spasmodically. The entire chamber was crawling back to life. Dust began to trickle from the ceiling.

Gwen looked down at Jack, brushing grit from his forehead. He was still out cold.

'Do something,' Gwen told Ianto.

'Gun's empty,' Ianto gasped. His face was white, his lips grey. 'Can't feel… anything…'

'Ianto!'

He keeled forward, losing consciousness. His hands were shaking, and his legs began to tremble as if his whole body had entered into some kind of fit.

'Assassin,' croaked Jack. His eyes flickered open, sore and narrow.

'What do you mean?'

Jack heaved himself upright, shaking his head. The right side of his face and neck was crimson. 'It's the assassin they sent for me,' he said, crawling over to where Ianto lay. 'It got Ianto by mistake.'

He rolled Ianto over onto his back and loosened his tie.

'I don't understand,' said Gwen. 'What assassin?'

'We got it wrong,' Jack explained heavily. 'The Hokrala didn't send a man with a gun. They knew that wouldn't work against me. So they sent a different kind of assassin.'

He pulled Ianto's tie free and ripped open his shirt, pulling the material away from his chest and stomach. The rashes had turned from a livid red to black.

Black that was moving.

Gwen's hand went to her mouth as realisation struck. Patches of Ianto's skin were covered with tiny, glistening black insects. They were burrowing away at the flesh, eating down through the skin. Many of them were fat with blood, their segmented bodies taut and glossy.

'Xilobytes,' said Jack, his mouth turning down with revulsion. A sob broke through his words. 'They must have been in the writ – just a few microscopic larvae. You couldn't see them with the naked eye but they were there – probably hidden in the watermark. They must have got onto Ianto's skin and got to work. They eat through human flesh, growing all the time, excreting a powerful local anaesthetic. He wouldn't have felt anything but an itch. They're feeding and multiplying, and if we don't do something they'll eat him right through to the bone.'

'But... what can we do?'

Jack took in a deep, shuddering breath. 'There's only one way to stop them – it's risky, though. You have to wait for them to get big enough and then pick them off with your fingers one by one and kill 'em.' To demonstrate, he chose one of the fattest insects and pulled it out of the wound. It left a bright spot of red where it had been.

Jack threw the wriggling creature on the floor and squashed it under his boot. Then he looked up at Gwen and met her eyes. 'Think you can do that?'

She shook her head, horrified.

'Then I'll do it,' Jack said. 'But that means you're gonna have to deal with Frank.'

Gwen looked back up at the casket. The tubes were flexing like the legs of some giant mutant spider. Frank Morgan's skull was still talking, but she hadn't heard a word of it in the last few minutes.

'Is there anybody there? I can hear voices. Where are you?'

He was growing more agitated, and his voice had descended to a deep, inhuman growl. As she watched, the dried skin that covered his eye sockets was suddenly forced apart as he opened his eyes for the first time in decades. Two darkened eyes forced their way through the dry folds of skin, swivelling madly, covered in bulging red veins. The eyes seemed to lock onto Gwen.

'Is that you, Gwen?'

'You gotta kill him,' Jack told her urgently. 'Now!' He picked another couple of Xilobytes out of Ianto's wounds and crushed them.

Gwen picked up Jack's revolver and aimed the heavy gun at Frank's open head. 'How will that help?' she asked. 'He's already dead. Half his head's missing for God's sake. He's just a load of dried-up flesh and bone!'

'He's the Undertaker,' Jack insisted. 'He's the control element of the time fissure. I know he's already dead. He was put there by the Already Dead. There's nothing they don't know about that sort of thing. Kill him – *now*.'

'Gwen? Is that you? Are you there?' Frank's reedy voice grated on her nerves. 'You're the only friendly voice I've heard in ages, Gwen. Don't tell me you've gone.'

'I'm here,' Gwen heard herself say, still aiming the Webley.

'And what about the yank? Captain Whatsisname? Is he here too?'

'Yes.'

'Do us a favour, love, and get us out of here…'

Jack reached up and grabbed Gwen's hand. 'Do it now!'

'I can't!' Gwen wailed. 'I can't shoot him, Jack. He's a human being, a person. It's murder.'

'You said yourself, he's already dead!'

'But he's not, is he? Listen to him, Jack!'

Jack looked imploringly at her. 'He's one life, Gwen. A life that should never have lived like this. If you don't kill him now then thousands – millions – of people are gonna die!'

'I can't do it, Jack.'

'You must!'

Frank's voice wheezed out of the darkness. 'Gwen? Jack? What's happening? I feel strange… so strange…'

Gwen let go of the gun with a cry.

And then, for Jack Harkness, it all seemed to fall into place. The dreams, nightmares, about Gwen – future echoes distorted by the Rift and his own subconscious: warning him that it would come to this. A choice between one life and millions, a choice Gwen Cooper could not be expected to make. The responsibility would be his, and his alone. Destruction on a scale unheard of, death upon death, millions of lives lost. A world of suffering.

Unless he did something.

Jack looked down at Ianto. He was unconscious, the alien insects chewing their way through his body with every passing second.

A choice between one life and millions.

No choice.

With a deep groan of anguish, Jack left Ianto and picked up the Webley. He straightened up and extended his arm. He narrowed one eye and lined up the V of the pistol's rear sight with the blade on the tip of the barrel. He wasn't going to miss this time. A .38 calibre bullet would shatter that brittle old skull like an antique vase from this range.

Carefully, deliberately, Jack gently squeezed the trigger.

And the gun clicked on empty.

LAST RITES

FORTY-SIX

For a long, disbelieving second Jack stood there, ramrod straight, gun still extended. Impotent. He realised then that the weight of the revolver was all wrong – too light for it to be loaded with anything but empty cartridges. In the excitement he had overlooked that simple fact.

Then the end of the world began.

The skull jerked and opened its jaws wide as a long, desperate shriek broke loose. The blackened tongue shrank back into the throat as Frank Morgan's remains seemed to deflate, almost as if the final scream was all that was left inside him. The parchment skin covering his head stretched and tore open, shrivelling like paper in a fire. The stringy flesh inside withered and crumbled and the dark, bulging eyes drew back into their sockets like snails into their shells. In less than ten seconds all that remained of Frank was a wrinkled, shrunken nut of matter and the long echo of his final cries.

The ground started to shake. Dust and bricks clattered from the ceiling, exploding on the floor.

'What's happening?' Gwen groaned, hanging on to Jack as the quake grew in intensity.

Tubes and wires snapped and lashed through the darkness like steel hawsers. 'End of the world,' Jack said. 'Temporal fusion.'

Ianto groaned, still alive, and for that Jack was profoundly grateful. He didn't want any of them to die down here. Not like this.

'Help me!' Jack bent down, slung one of Ianto's arms over his shoulders and hoisted him up.

Limping badly, Gwen got herself under Ianto's other arm and helped Jack manoeuvre him through the door. Bricks and mortar poured down behind them, creating a thick cloud of choking dust.

The ground was shaking so hard it was almost impossible to walk, especially supporting Ianto. They tumbled from side to side as they staggered through the passages, tripping over broken masonry and the bodies of fallen pallbearers. Gwen's ankle couldn't take the strain and she collapsed with an agonised, despairing yell.

'Keep moving!' roared Jack. He picked her up by the scruff of her jacket, grabbed her around the waist with his free arm and then carried on. He could barely walk carrying both Gwen and Ianto, but he had to get out. If he was going to face the end of the world he wanted to do it outside, where he could see it coming and meet it head on. Not trapped underground.

There was a deep, deafening noise filling the passages now, rising inexorably from what felt like the depths of the Earth. The quake grew more violent, and the brickwork over their heads began to split apart, as if struck by a giant axe from above. Bricks and soil dropped through the breach, almost burying them. With a strength lent to her by sheer terror, Gwen scrabbled through the debris and clawed her way towards the light above. Jack pushed her on, shouting at her to move, urging her upwards through the tumbling earth.

She broke free a second later, spitting soil and grit, climbing up through a river of shale. The slope levelled out and she turned, reaching back for Jack. He held Ianto up to her and she grabbed his hands, dragging him out of the chasm. Jack crawled up after them and heaved himself out onto the ground.

The earthquake rumbled on.

Jack knelt by Gwen and Ianto, his arms around them, holding them close enough to feel their hearts beating. His own heart thudded wildly against his chest as he took in their new surroundings.

'It really is the end of the world,' breathed Gwen. Her eyes were wide, terrified. Jack squeezed her tightly.

The church was crumbling, great chunks of brickwork collapsing as the building shook and sank into the quaking earth. The ground all around them was an uneven mass of paving flags and soil, as if the Black House had been transformed into a bomb site. Beyond that the railings and trees were twisted and broken; beyond those were the houses. Roofs buckled and collapsed, walls broke down, clouds of dust rose into the air along with screams and sobs of the people inside.

Police and ambulance sirens wailed a terrible lament as the destruction spread, accompanied by the slow, relentless rumble of the quake.

'What have we done?' moaned Gwen. 'What have we done?'

'I've failed,' Jack said quietly. 'Just like Hokrala said I would.'

FORTY-SEVEN

They crouched beneath a storm, lightning flaring and crackling with sudden fury. Jack put his arms around them and held them close as he looked up to heaven with tears in his eyes.

'What have I done?' he asked.

'It was me,' Gwen said miserably. 'It's all my fault. I couldn't pull the trigger when it mattered. I let this happen.'

Jack looked down at her, squeezed her. 'No,' he insisted. 'I should never have asked that of you. There was nothing you could have done – this was all started by the pallbearers, remember.'

Gwen let out a sob, although the enormity of it all prevented any tears. 'Rhys… Oh, Rhys…'

The sky above them swirled with dark, clotted clouds. Lightning flashed.

Jack opened the cover on his leather wrist-strap to check the readings. Coloured lights flashed manically and he forced himself to concentrate, to understand what was happening. It was the only way he could cope.

'It's a temporal fissure,' he reported. His lips felt numb as he talked, and he had to raise his voice to be heard over the storm. 'The Rift is being forced open, wider, much wider. It's disintegrating the planet from here outwards.'

'How long have we got?'

'Can't say.' Jack made some adjustments to the manipulator. 'At the moment the destruction is localised – central Cardiff only. But it's spreading every moment. It'll gather momentum, destroying this city first, then the coastline. Then England, Europe… There will be tidal waves and seismic shockwaves so massive they will break the planet into pieces.'

'Then this is it.' Gwen grabbed Jack's arm. 'This really is the end.'

Tears streamed from Jack's eyes and he cupped one hand around her face. 'I'm sorry.'

Ianto was stirring. 'I take it… things haven't improved…'

'Easy, Ianto.' Jack rested a hand against his forehead. 'Easy.'

Ianto's body was covered in dust and grime, but the wounds on his chest were still starkly visible, still crawling with Xilobytes. Angrily, Gwen reached down and flicked one of the largest away.

'Why is the sky green?' Ianto asked.

They looked up. Dark clouds swirled like the eye of a storm, and a dull, angry green light shone from within.

'Oh God,' Gwen murmured.

Jack took another reading on his wrist device. 'Time flux. Something's breaking through the Rift. Something big…'

The sky suddenly warped and split, as if something massive had pressed against the fabric of the universe and forced it open. The green-black clouds broiled and raged, but a narrow strip of orange light had appeared in the centre. It widened, like an opening eye, and a fierce, flickering yellow light shone down.

'What is it?'

'I have no idea.' Jack's wrist strap bleeped and he checked it again. 'Something's wrong…'

'Seriously?' said Ianto.

'I mean different,' Jack said, frowning. 'The fissure's getting wider but this is something else.'

Slowly Jack got to his feet, looking directly up at the shimmering bulge in the sky. It was changing colour, swirling with deep blood red, then purple, green, pink, like oil spilled in water. Electric forces crackled around the edges, discharging to the crumbling earth below in bright, jagged flashes. A harsh wind blew Jack's greatcoat and hair as he gazed up into the glowing eye of the storm. His eyes were shining with a sudden understanding.

'I don't want to die…' Ianto said weakly.

Jack turned back to them. 'You're not going to,' he said forcefully. 'Not if I can help it.'

He started to move away, and Gwen jumped up, grabbing his arm. 'Where are you going?'

'There's no time to explain!' Jack had to shout above the sound of the quake, the sirens, and the fierce, galvanistic crackle of the lightning storm. His face was bathed in a golden glow from above, and Gwen could see that his eyes were suddenly full of purpose. 'Stay here. Look after Ianto.'

'But I don't want you to go!'

'I've got to! It's our only chance!' He pushed her away. 'Stay with Ianto. I'll be back!'

And with that he was gone, running, coat flying out behind him. Gwen watched him bound over the tumbledown rocks and earth and then there was a lightning strike and, when the flash had faded from her eyes, he was gone.

FORTY-EIGHT

Jack stumbled over the broken land until he reached the SUV. The car was shaking as the ground beneath it heaved with each successive quake, but it was still serviceable. He wrenched open the door and climbed inside, starting the engine with trembling fingers. A massive shockwave rocked the vehicle, and Jack caught his breath. There would be more quakes, each worse than the previous one, building to a crescendo as the surrounded landmass caved in to the temporal fissure. Huge cracks were opening up in the ground, filled with a deep, crimson glow.

But the SUV was built for conditions like this: rough terrain was no problem for the heavy, turbo-charged four-wheel drive. He hit the accelerator, and the car bounced across the buckling road surface, crashing over a fallen wall at the edge of the Black House.

The streets were alive with people and cars, panicking, looking for a way to escape. Horns blared and police cars whipped up and down, flickering blue lights picking out the piles of rubble and furniture that had once been flats and houses. People were shouting and crying, dogs howling, and all against the background wail of emergency sirens.

Jack had to ignore them all.

He tooled the SUV carefully through the busier areas, grinding his teeth with impatience as people drifted aimlessly across the road. Some of them held children and babies, and looked at Jack through the windscreen with a mixture of fear and resentment as he drove past.

Many roads were already unusable. Buildings had collapsed and thrown debris across them, trees had fallen, and one major carriageway into town was clogged with a giant vehicle pile-up. Cars and vans were lodged nose-to-tail, crumpled, useless, gouts of steam drifting up into the churning green sky. Inside the SUV, Jack was saved having to listen to the cries of the trapped and wounded, and he let the emergency services deal with it as best they could. Two ambulances were trying to nudge their way through the traffic, lights and sirens virtually useless. The situation had spiralled out of their control in a matter of minutes and he guessed most of the blues-and-twos were driving around randomly, as confused and panic-stricken as everybody else.

He slung the SUV onto Eastern Avenue, heading south towards the city centre and put his foot down. He had to swerve to avoid the bigger fissures that kept cracking open every few seconds. Whatever route he took, he was going to need help.

He took a spare earpiece out of the glove compartment, driving one-handed. He clipped it to his ear and then punched a speed-dial button on the dashboard. Within a few seconds he was connected to the central South Wales Police communications network. It was busy, but the Torchwood SUV carried an automatic override.

'This is South Wales Police,' said a recorded voice. 'We are currently experiencing a very busy period. Your call is in a queue to be answered. Please hold or otherwise try again later.'

'This is Captain Jack Harkness. Torchwood security clearance four slash seven-four three-one-seven. Put me through to Detective Kathy Swanson.'

The line crackled, and fifteen seconds later Kathy Swanson's voice filled his ear. She sounded suitably stressed. 'God help me, Harkness, but this had better be bloody good or the next time I see you, I'll have your balls for breakfast.'

'Promises, promises,' said Jack, but his heart wasn't in it.

'Tell me this is Torchwood business,' said Swanson, 'because I really can't believe we've just been hit by an earthquake. Not even Cardiff could be that unlucky.'

'It's kind of Torchwood business, yeah.'

'Kind of?'

'No time for details, Kathy. I need your help. I'm on Eastern Avenue. I've got to get back to Roald Dahl Plass and the roads are all screwed going into the city from the north east. If you're still in contact with any patrol cars out there, then clear a route for me, will you?'

'Are you *serious*?' Swanson's voice rose shrilly and he winced. 'We are up to our eyes in emergency calls. The switchboard's jammed. The army's on standby. Cardiff Emergency Management Unit at City Hall is in full session as we speak. We don't know whether to evacuate the city or not – and frankly, if the order came through for that then I don't think we could actually do it. And *you* want a bloody *police escort*?'

The line crackled with interference and Jack lost most of what came then, but he guessed it was largely expletives. When she came back online, Swanson was still in midstream: '... son of a bitch if you think...'

'All right, can it.'

'You'd better be on top of this soon, Jack!' Her voice was trembling, and he guessed that Swanson was as scared as anybody.

'Sure,' he lied. 'But I've gotta move fast.'

'I can't give you an escort, but I'll try and get whatever cars we have to keep some routes free.'

'It's appreciated.'

'Try and get onto the Pen-y-Lan road. It's the clearest due to the roadworks.'

'Great, thanks.' Jack glanced out of the window, got his bearings, threw the SUV into a tight left-hand turn, bumping over a mini roundabout.

There was the briefest pause, and Jack could imagine Swanson sitting in the operations room at Police HQ, a hand to her brow, perspiring. Then the question: 'Jack – what's happening? Just tell me.'

Jack bit his lip and closed the call. He took a detour, longer than he had hoped because of the spreading devastation, and headed for the southbound roads. He was racing an expanding tide of destruction and losing. The traffic heading out of the centre of Cardiff had overcome the capacity of the roads and ground to a standstill. Jack was forced to thread his way through backstreets and rat runs, driving over central reservations and pavements and at one point barrelling down the wrong side of an empty dual carriageway. He had the SUV blue lights flashing but there were so many emergency vehicles around that they counted for little.

He sent the SUV straight over another roundabout, bouncing it until the shock absorbers began to protest a little too much. On the far side a minibus swerved in front of him and he stood on the breaks, the SUV tyres locking hard and dragging a black line of scorched rubber across the road and pavement. The minibus sounded its horn, its driver raising a fist at Jack, but he was already on his way.

Jack reduced speed as he approached a section of road between two rows of high street shops. The tarmac was buckled and split, water from a broken main spurting high into the air and drenching the men who were systematically breaking shop windows and stealing whatever they could lay their hands on. Jack gritted his teeth, filled with rage. Couldn't these people see that the world was ending around them? What use was a plasma

TV and a microwave going to be to them now? If they survived the next twenty-four hours, they would be looking for food to steal, fighting with their neighbours for a loaf of bread and a tin of beans.

Survival would belong to those who could fight. It was a chilling thought.

He had to carry on.

At the end of the street he pulled out into a clear area and increased speed. Someone hurled a brick at him and it bounced off the rear window. Jack shook his head in despair and headed for the centre of town. He put his foot down, pushing the SUV as fast as it would go. A policeman flashed past, shouting something, but he took no notice. Hopefully Kathy Swanson had got the message through and he was just waving the SUV on.

There were more people up ahead, civilians, signalling him to stop.

Jack hauled the steering wheel around and took the next turning. It was a narrow side street, not far from Taff Road. Not a great place to be, and certainly not on the brink of doom. Dark figures milled around the road up ahead. The narrow road was full of shadows, hemmed in on either side by tall buildings as the black clouds above. He turned on the SUV headlamps and the beams picked out a crouched, snarling figure in front.

Weevil.

They'd sensed the destruction above, felt the earthquake deep in their underground nests. Hungry and frightened, they had been forced to the surface.

Jack caught a glimpse of the bestial red eyes beneath the furrowed brows, the sharp, toxic fangs glinting in his headlights. He accelerated and the Weevil disappeared under the SUV with a heavy crunch. No time to stop now, and if any Weevil stumbled across a human being it would attack and kill.

There were more Weevils ahead. The nest must have

been nearby, probably in the basement of one of the disused warehouses that littered the area. The Weevils snarled and spat at the SUV as it whipped past them, swerving in and out. He clipped one, spinning it away, and then hit another full on – for a few moments it clung to the radiator, sprawled across the SUV's bonnet. It roared, angry little eyes fixing on Jack, but then it lost its grip, sliding down the bonnet leaving a trail of scratches from its claws, until it went under. The SUV bounced over it, but then the tyres suddenly lost traction, and Jack felt the vehicle spin around as he exited the road at the far end.

He wrestled with the wheel as the SUV slewed from side to side. The wheels screeched. Jack strained to bring it under control and as he did so he saw a woman straight ahead, caught square in his headlights. There was a look of sudden fear in her wide blue eyes that would stay with Jack for ever – the terrible certainty that four tons of Sports Utility Vehicle were about to flatten her.

With a yell, Jack tore the steering wheel to the left, sending the SUV into a sudden, neck-wrenching swerve. He was thrown against the door as the car tipped over on two wheels with a roar of protest. And then the vehicle was hurtling down a shallow embankment, smashing through a pair of parked cars and spinning out of control.

The windscreen shattered, exploding through the cabin and Jack ducked as the SUV ploughed sideways into a shop front with a screech of tearing metal and splintering wood.

The SUV rocked to a halt. Dazed, covered in broken glass, Jack opened the door and climbed out. He emerged onto the street, his vision blurred and his ears ringing. He could taste blood in his mouth.

Someone shouted at him. He looked up, focused and saw a woman. The same woman he'd nearly flattened seconds before. She was calling out to him, and behind her, lumbering along in its simian fashion, was a Weevil.

Jack felt for his Webley – it wasn't in the holster.

The Weevil was almost on the woman now. It was growling, fangs bared, reaching out for her with curled talons. She was screaming and running for her life, fully aware of the danger.

Jack's hand found the knife almost at the same time he remembered it, nestled safely in its protective sheath inside his coat pocket. It was the AI throwing-knife – its telepathic trintillium blade designed for moments like this. He drew back his hand and hurled the blade with all the forced he could muster. It only had to be in the right general direction – his thoughts would do the rest.

The steel flashed through the air, swerving past the woman to hit the Weevil square between the eyes with an audible thud. It straightened, mouth hanging open, the hilt protruding from its head. Then the Weevil fell backwards, like an axed tree, and lay dead in the middle of the road.

The woman let out a cry of relief. She turned to thank the stranger in the long coat – but he had already gone.

FORTY-NINE

Gwen Cooper knew the end was near. The ground shook beneath her, all around her was destruction and, above, the skies swirled menacingly. But she was still alive and so was Ianto, and at the moment that was all she could rely on.

She clung on to that thought and tried her best to blank out everything else: Rhys, friends, family, colleagues. Places and things she took for granted in her home city had to be shut out of her mind. She had to concentrate on the here and now, on herself and Ianto – as far as she could tell, the last two living people for miles around. The police sirens were distant now, whispers only, barely audible over the constant background rumble of the quake.

An amber light suffused the entire area. Above them, the inky green sky bulged and the swirling fire continued to burn inside. Lightning crackled down in flickering lines, drawing sparks wherever it touched. The air tasted of electricity, a sharp, tingling in the mouth that set the nerves on edge.

'What's happening…?' Ianto's voice was barely a croak.

Gwen looked at him and shook her head, lost for words.

Ianto lay propped up against a huge piece of masonry that

had sunk halfway into the crypt below. His skin was white but he was hot, fevered, his skin running with sweat. His eyes rolled beneath flickering eyelids.

The wounds on his chest and stomach looked red and sore, peppered with wriggling Xilobytes. Gwen gritted her teeth, reached for the largest and pulled it off. Ianto gave a little groan as the thing came free, its tiny jaws tearing another little piece of flesh away. Grimacing, Gwen threw the insect on the ground and flattened it with a loose brick she had chosen for the purpose. Its underside was sticky with pulped remains.

Ianto's eyes opened and he looked down at his chest. 'What… what are you doing?'

'Don't look,' Gwen advised him. 'Close your eyes and rest.'

'What… what are they?' He frowned, trying to focus on his sores. Gradually realisation dawned. 'What the hell…?'

'Lie still,' Gwen said tersely. She had to be firm, confident, show no sign of the bubbling revulsion that was building inside her.

'What are they?' Ianto's breathing began ragged as he began to squirm with panic, his eyes fixated on the insects.

'Xilobyte assassins,' Gwen told him. 'Meant for Jack. They missed.'

Ianto's head lolled back and he moaned out loud. 'Get them off me!'

'I'm trying to. Now lie still.'

She picked another one off and squashed it with the brick.

'How… how many more are there?' Ianto asked.

'I can't tell. A few.' Gwen bit her lip. Every time she pulled one free, she glimpsed another, half-immersed in Ianto's blood. She hadn't allowed herself to try and count them; instead she was focusing on dealing with just one at a time. Eventually, she knew, she would reach the end. And that would be good for Ianto – but what then? *Then* she would have to face up to what was happening around them. And at the moment she could not even allow herself to consider that prospect for a single second.

'Where's Jack?'

'He's… gone.'

'Gone where?'

'For help.' She didn't know if this was true or not, but what else could she say? And when she glanced into Ianto's eyes, she knew that he doubted her. What help could there possibly be now?

'Has… has he run away?'

She shook her head. 'Of course not. Jack wouldn't do that.'

But now she wouldn't even look at Ianto's eyes, in case he saw the doubt in hers. What did they really know about Jack Harkness? He was full of secrets, a lifetime of changes and escapes and adventures. Who was to say that he wasn't going to escape from this by the skin of his teeth? That wrist-strap of his – they had seen it used as a personal teleport once, in the direst of emergencies. He'd left them on their own then, to defend the Hub against the worst of enemies. But what now?

Gwen knew that Ianto was thinking the same things. She stole a glance at him, and his eyes met hers. They were red and running with tears.

'Do you think he'd leave us?' she heard herself ask. 'Like this?'

He shook his head. 'No.'

'Me neither. So let's get to work.' She yanked another Xilobyte off his chest and killed it.

They heard a dog barking close by and the sudden noise startled them both. They hadn't realised how quiet everything had become. It was almost as if the whole world was holding its breath; there was the low, background rumble from deep beneath them and the occasional crackle of lightning, but apart from that a weird silence had slowly built up.

The dog sounded agitated, almost frightened, and no wonder. Something like this would cause panic among animals used to the natural order of things. They had no knowledge of time rifts or temporal fusion bombs.

The barking increased, became a frightened yelp, and was suddenly overtaken by a throaty, crunching growl and then silence.

Gwen and Ianto looked at each other.

'That didn't sound good,' Gwen whispered.

'Look!' Ianto jerked a hand up, pointing. 'What's that?'

Gwen looked and saw a hideous creature crawling over the ruins of the Black House on short, powerful legs. It was reptilian as far as she could tell, shaped like a giant toad and with a wide mouth full of something covered in ragged fur. The toad creature opened its jaws and dropped the dead animal on the ground. With a start, Gwen realised it was an Alsatian dog – its black and tan fur stained with blood. Red saliva drooled from the toad-creature's jagged fangs and its little black eyes blinked evilly at her over the corpse.

'Just when you think things can't get any worse,' she muttered.

'It's coming for us,' Ianto said. He tried to push back with his legs, but in truth he was too weak and there was nowhere to go.

'It's a pitbullfrog,' Gwen realised. 'Jack said there was one still loose in the city.'

'And we've found it,' Ianto said. 'Aren't we the lucky ones.'

'Actually… I think it's found us.'

And with an angry, blood-curdling snarl the pitbullfrog leapt towards them.

FIFTY

The motorbike was a 250cc trail bike with high suspension and a well-worn saddle. Jack had found it lying on its side, abandoned by its rider. Never one to look a gift horse in the mouth, Jack had used his wrist-strap manipulator to hot-wire the bike and was now riding it hard towards Roald Dahl Plass.

It was perfect for this terrain – broken, ragged tarmac strewn with lumps of fallen masonry and crashed vehicles. Fires had taken hold across the city and thick black palls of smoke drifted through the ruins. The level of destruction reminded him of London during the Blitz.

Part of his mind turned that fact over: how had it come to this, in Cardiff, now? All it needed were some Luftwaffe bombers droning overhead with a couple of Messerschmitt squadrons for protection. And yet this damage was, to all intents and purposes, self-inflicted.

He had to banish all such thoughts from his mind and concentrate. He stood high in the saddle, letting the bike take the impacts as the wheels bounced and jerked over the rubble. The engine growled and roared alternatively, depending on whether he was squeezing the throttle or the brakes.

Not far now.

His earpiece buzzed – an unusual signal, it wasn't Ianto or Gwen. Then there was a sharp crackle in his ear that made him jerk his head to one side and an unfamiliar voice:

'… is Captain Erisa Magambo of the Unified Intelligence Taskforce… Priority Red Alpha call to Captain Jack—'

'Erisa!' exclaimed Jack. He had to shout over the roar of the motorbike. 'I'm a bit busy right now…'

'I'm sure. This is UNIT HQ London – we're getting some very alarming reports from our geostationary satellites over South Wales, Captain, and I can't raise any of my agents in Cardiff. Care to elucidate?'

'Nothing doing here, ma'am,' Jack yelled. 'Just routine Torchwood business, no need for UNIT to get involved.'

'Really? That engine noise – is that a motorbike you're riding, Captain?'

'Yes, ma'am!'

An audible sigh. 'On your way to save the world single-handed, no doubt.'

'You said it.'

'I don't need to remind you, Captain Harkness, of the trouble I could cause both you and your organisation if I discovered that you were in any way responsible for any long-term or irreparable damage to the planet…'

'Did I ever tell you how much I love a woman in uniform, Captain?'

A hesitation. 'Er – I believe so, yes, once.'

'Geneva, wasn't it?' Jack revved the engine hard, swerving the bike through a slalom of debris on Lloyd George Avenue. 'The summer of 2002.'

'Um, that's right, yes…'

'Ah – I remember it well! You wore black combat fatigues and a red beret.' Jack could see the Millennium Centre shining ahead of him and gunned the accelerator.

'And you were wearing that old greatcoat…'

'Oh, I really dig those red berets!'

'Captain Harkness, I do believe you would flirt with the last person on Earth given half a chance.'

The bike skidded to a halt on Road Dahl Plass and Jack dismounted on the run, leaving the machine to clatter to the ground behind him. He sprinted for the central water tower. 'Keep shining those buttons, ma'am. Gotta go.'

He reached the tower and hit the control on his wrist-strap that would operate the paving-stone lift. His earcom crackled again: 'Whatever it is you're doing, Harkness – and the Lord only knows what's going on there – do it fast.'

'Wilco that.' The lift began to descend.

'Good luck and Godspeed, Captain.'

FIFTY-ONE

Gwen swung the house brick with all her strength as the pitbullfrog closed in. She'd had the brick in her hand since smashing the last Xilobyte and using it now was instinctive.

A lucky strike, maybe, but it worked. The brick crunched heavily into the creature's bulbous left eye, bursting it like a soft-boiled egg. The frog squealed and practically turned a somersault with the pain, thrashing its thick head from side to side in a frenzy as it landed.

There was no other weapon available. Gwen raised the brick over her head and then threw it, hoping another hard knock might scare the thing away completely. But this blow was less effective, bouncing off the warty hide with a soft thud.

The tough little brute had recovered with phenomenal speed. It squatted in front of Gwen, panting, its sharp little fangs bared and drooling. There was an ugly mess where its eye had been, the socket full of ichor. The creature kept shaking its head as if trying to shrug off the pain, spraying blood high into the air.

'OK,' breathed Gwen, struggling to stay calm. Her heart was pounding painfully inside her ribs. 'OK…'

'Ankle…' croaked Ianto from behind her.

'What?'

The pitbullfrog screamed and leapt at her in that moment, jaws snapping. She jerked away, rolling, felt her elbow glance off its jaw, then the sharp snagging of its teeth in the sleeve of her leather jacket. It bit deeply, missing her flesh, but securing a good grip on the tough material so that she couldn't hope to break free. Then it began to shake her like a terrier with a rat.

She kicked and struggled and twisted and turned, gasping, crying, trying to shake it loose but only too aware that the moment she broke free it would be on her properly, astride her, bringing those razor-sharp fangs down for the killer bite on her neck.

Then there was a loud boom – a gunshot – and the pitbullfrog shook like it had been kicked, hard, right up the arse. It squirmed for a second, allowed its jaws to gape, letting go of Gwen's sleeve. She scrambled away and turned to see Ianto holding a small automatic, the barrel smoking. His trouser leg was pulled up to reveal a smart ankle-holster.

Aware of the danger, the pitbullfrog manoeuvred itself around to face Ianto. Gwen saw a huge, ragged tear in its backside where the bullet had struck. Blood was pulsing out in time to the beat of whatever alien heart pumped inside.

Ianto shot it again – once, twice, three times, each successive bullet driving the creature back another metre and forcing it to writhe and snap. It wasn't until the fourth round entered the ruins of its left eye and blew its tiny brain out of the side of its skull that the frog finally gave up and lay still.

Ianto's hand was shaking. He dropped the pistol and sank back against the wall.

Gwen crawled across to him, avoiding the widening pool of blood around the pitbullfrog.

'Ankle-holster,' she said. 'Good one.'

'No well-dressed man… should be without one.'

She laughed. Ianto's suit jacket had been left behind in the crypt, his white shirt lay in tatters around his chest, and he was covered in grime and blood.

'Now where the hell were we?' she asked, peering at the wounds on his torso.

He closed his eyes. 'I'd rather not think about it,' he said. 'Just do what you have to do.'

She clenched her jaws and picked off the remaining Xilobytes as quickly as she could. Her fingers were slippery and the last couple seemed to want to cling on for dear life, as if sensing the danger. One of them buried itself deeper to escape, almost disappearing in a finger-sized well of blood.

'I can't reach the last one,' said Gwen.

'Back trouser pocket,' Ianto gasped.

Obediently Gwen tried the pocket, forcing Ianto to twist himself uncomfortably around. He groaned with the effort. Eventually Gwen found a Swiss Army Knife and pulled it free.

'Boy scout?' she asked. She opened one of the blades and found the entry hole in Ianto's stomach. It was sticky with blood, but there was no sign of the insect.

'Inside,' grunted Ianto.

Gwen peered more closely.

'Cut it out if you have to,' Ianto said quickly.

Gwen tore of a strip of his shirt and took a pen out of his jacket pocket. She wound the material around the pen and then gave it to him to bite on, wedging it between his teeth. 'It's going to hurt.'

Ianto gave her a 'really?' look and then closed his eyes.

Carefully, Gwen inserted the blade into the wound. The metal sliced the skin and Ianto's stomach quivered as he tensed. A hard groan of pain forced its way past the gag.

Gritting her teeth almost as hard as Ianto was, Gwen tried to feel for the Xilobyte with the penknife. Ianto's face was purple, the veins standing out on his forehead. She dug deeper, felt him jerk and whimper again.

Concentrating, Gwen slid the knife in further. Something moved against the tip of the blade, something hard. It was the insect, wriggling inside the hole it had eaten.

It couldn't go any further now. It was trapped. Desperately it tried to burrow deeper, but Gwen twisted the blade, felt it dig into the insect, and then pulled slowly backwards, maintaining the pressure on the creature so as not to lose it. Ianto threw back his head, spitting the pen out with an almighty howl of protest. Gwen almost lost it as he convulsed, but then she saw the first of its legs squirming in the pool of blood that had formed around the hole. She dragged the insect out, watching in revulsion as it tried to keep a grip with its many wavering legs and failed. The tip of the knife was buried in the creature's underside. The legs scrabbled at the blade as she pulled it free, turned quickly and drove it deep into the ground nearby. Skewered, the Xilobyte finally stopped moving.

Ianto's scream had faded to a terrible moan. Gwen made a pad out of the remains of his shirt and jammed it against the bubbling hole in his stomach. She felt faint but utterly relieved.

'You're done,' she gasped, exhausted. She sank down next to him and put her arm around him.

It was several seconds before he could speak again. His words sounded strained, but she could hear the old Ianto. Just. 'Is it just me…' he began, 'or is it getting quieter?'

They listened. The ground was still rumbling beneath them, but it almost felt as if the earthquake had been put on hold. Gwen frowned. 'Maybe it's building up to the big one,' she said quietly, holding him closer. She was cold now, shivering as the shock caught up with her now the immediate adrenalin-firing crisis was over. Now all there was to face was total destruction.

And yet it seemed to be hesitating.

They looked up at the coruscating orange bulge in the sky above, still wondering if this was some unknown phenomenon resulting from the temporal fusion blast. But something was changing. The air smelled sharply of ozone and the lightning flashes were growing more frequent, and more violent. They hadn't noticed during the fight with the pitbullfrog but the discharging electricity had begun to form a flickering wall of light around the entire area.

'I've no idea what that thing is,' Ianto said. 'But it's getting impatient.'

FIFTY-TWO

The entire coastal area had suffered a tremendous seismic upheaval after the temporal fusion detonation, and the shockwaves had been felt acutely in the harbour area. Jack had seen the water in the bay heaving, thirty-metre waves rolling up to the front and exploding in gigantic white geysers. The sea-spray was blowing inland, leaving his face stinging and the taste of salt on his lips.

It was spectacularly frightening, but not as frightening as the sight that met him as the paving-stone descended.

The Hub had been crunched, and badly. There was hardly anything here Jack recognised: just a shambles of twisted metal and flames.

The elevator was working, and that was about all. Jack stepped off the platform, kicking aside some fallen steelwork and trying not to look too hard at the mess. There was dust, masonry, metal and broken glass everywhere, with sparks flying from all the workstations in sharp, actinic flashes.

He felt a great knot of grief forming in his chest but he couldn't afford to get emotional now.

The tears were caused by the smoke, that was all.

He passed the mangled remains of Gwen's workstation. The screens were still flickering as the computers fought to stay online – they were tough, all right, built to last. *Just like me*, he thought grimly. But at least it meant there was still power running somewhere; there were plenty of back-up generators in the Hub in case of emergency.

His boots crunched over an avalanche of broken glass and pot plants; all that remained of the Hot House. He stepped across the shallow water course which ran around the base of the Rift Manipulator and headed for the cells.

There was plenty of smoke down here, thick, rolling, oily clouds of it. Something in the lower levels was burning badly. Coughing and retching, Jack staggered towards the detention cells.

He stopped in front of Cell One, gasping for breath. The clear plastic door was warped and cloudy, buckling in the heat as he watched. And behind it stood Zero.

Not sitting.

Standing.

Waiting for him.

'I knew it,' Jack yelled. He raised a boot and kicked at the plastic door. It was weakened, useless now, and it only took three heavy blows to knock it out of its frame.

'Time to go,' Jack told the jelly creature.

It stood there impassively, staring at him. It still didn't have any eyes to speak of – no features at all – but Jack fancied the creature had assumed even more human-like proportions since he'd last seen it, and it really felt like the thing was looking at him.

Almost expectantly.

'Well, don't just stand there,' Jack said. 'Let's go.'

And then something huge and heavy hit Jack on the back of his head and he sprawled forward, stars exploding everywhere in his vision. He felt himself go down on his hands and knees, hard against the concrete, totally stunned.

Something – someone – had hit him from behind. He hadn't even known they were there. His vision was blurred and he thought he probably had a fractured skull. He could feel blood oozing out of his scalp into his hair.

'Got you now, human,' said a familiar, sneering voice.

Jack forced his eyes open, blinked to clear them, looked up at his assailant.

The leering Blowfish face spat at him. 'You're so gonna die now, bastard!'

Kerko launched a kick and there was a dull crack as one of Jack's ribs broke.

The foot was pulled back again, ready for another powerful kick.

Jack reached out instinctively, catching Kerko's foot on the next swing, yanking it sideways. There was a crash as the Blowfish hit the deck, but he was fast, rolling clear and jumping to his feet without hesitation.

Jack hauled himself up the wall. 'I really don't have time for this,' he growled.

'You don't have any choice.' Kerko's wide mouth twisted into a fishy grin. 'It's payback time, Harkness!' In the Blowfish's right hand was a small but lethal-looking knife.

'Listen, Kerko,' Jack began. It was painful to speak with a broken rib but he had to ignore it. 'There's more important things going on here than you and me. You can see the state of the place. It's havoc up there—' he jerked a thumb towards the ceiling '—but I'm trying to do something about it.'

'Yeah? Do something about *this*!' Kerko lunged forward, slashing wildly with the knife.

Jack jerked backwards as the blade whistled by, but Kerko had already started his back swing and before Jack could move again he felt the blade slit the skin of his left hand.

He pushed backwards, up the steps towards the Hub. Kerko

slashed again and Jack felt the tug of the steel through his greatcoat as he stumbled away.

The Blowfish was on him in an instant as they crashed into the main section of the Hub, switching his grip on the knife and shoving it up towards Jack's stomach as if he was trying to fillet him.

Which would be quite funny, Jack thought, if the situation wasn't so dire.

He kicked out, knocking Kerko sideways, and they circled each other carefully through the wreckage.

'The whole world's starting to burn up there,' Jack told him. 'I've got to stop it, Kerko. I *can* stop it. Just let me go now – and we'll settle this later.'

'Huh!' The Blowfish spat heavily at him. 'Don't think there's gonna be a later, Harkness. This scumball planet's going down and I really don't give a shit. But before it all goes, I'm gonna take you down first. For my brother!'

He lunged again, making lightning-fast swipes with the knife and Jack was suddenly dodging and ducking and feeling the blade biting again, but he ignored it, wrapping his own arm around Kerko's and twisting savagely. The Blowfish cried out and dropped the knife as Jack swung him around, smashing him into Ianto's workstation.

Kerko tried to climb free but Jack grabbed him with an angry snarl and slammed him into the coffee machine, sending cups and beans flying. They exchanged punches, fast, crunching jabs and rolled clear of the machine in a shower of spoons and serviettes. They rolled across the floor, each desperately searching for a grip on the other. Jack's fingers closed around a tea spoon and he plunged it deep into Kerko's head, but the handle missed anything vital and the fish didn't even seem to notice. He staggered backwards, throwing Jack away, the spoon protruding ludicrously from the top of his skull.

Jack was panting. 'Give it up, Kerko. I ain't got the time!'

Flames were crackling fiercely all around the Hub, computer screens burning and popping in great sparking flashes. There were power cables dangling from the roof, the ends fizzing with electricity.

'Look at this place,' jeered Kerko. 'What a bloody mess!' He let out a harsh laugh. 'I couldn't believe it when the quake came and my cell door bust open. It's destiny, Harkness, that's what it is. Destiny!'

'Says the guy with a spoon sticking out of his head.'

Kerko picked up a burning chair, hurling it at Jack. He ducked underneath and sprang, driving his head into the fish's solar plexus. They crashed over a desk and skidded across a carpet of broken glass. Jack scrambled to his feet, slipping and sliding on the glass, and then climbed up the railing to the next level.

Kerko raced after him, a burning, murderous light in his tiny black eyes.

FIFTY-THREE

Gwen and Ianto huddled together beneath the lowering sky. Black clouds were scudding around the shining, open wound above, and lightning crackled constantly around the edges. Long, wavering lines of light poured down from the edges like golden blood, spattering on the ground in brilliant sparks.

'If I wasn't so scared,' said Gwen, 'I might think this was quite beautiful.'

Ianto agreed. 'It's one hell of a light show for the end of the world.'

He was in a bad way. The wounds were still very raw, the pain had really begun to kick in now that the Xilobytes were gone and there was no anaesthetic. Gwen had tried to patch up the wounds as best she could with the remains of his shirt and jacket, but it was only a temporary job. He needed a hospital.

She watched his eyes close as his head sank back against the concrete. 'You OK?'

'Fine.' He was pale, he'd lost a lot of blood, and they were starting to get seriously cold. The perspiration from their fight with the pitbullfrog had long since evaporated, reducing their body temperature still further. Now the rain was starting to get heavier as the dark clouds circled lower and lower. Cold grey puddles of water were forming all around them.

'We need to get under cover,' Gwen said.

'I can't move,' Ianto told her. His voice sounded weak. 'It hurts too much.'

Gwen swore and looked around. There was no cover anywhere. The church was no more than a heap of rubble. They were crouched in the lee of a broken wall, but apart from that they were completely exposed.

Ianto was beginning to shiver, so Gwen took off her leather jacket and draped it over him. His hand gripped hers, and his skin felt horribly cold. She squeezed his hand and his eyes opened a fraction. They looked red and sore. He started to say something and Gwen had to lean in close to hear him.

'He will come back, won't he?'

'Of course he will.'

He was still looking at her. 'How do you know?'

'Because,' Gwen said in a small voice, 'he's Captain Jack.'

They lay together in silence then, as the rain water seeped through their clothes and the lightning crashed all around them, holding on to each other like frightened children in a storm.

FIFTY-FOUR

Jack and Kerko crashed into the hospital gurney, sending it spinning across the Autopsy Room. Caught in each other's murderous grip, they twisted and turned, wrestling for any kind of advantage. Trays of medical equipment clattered across the floor as they flung each other around the circular chamber like gladiators in a fighting pit.

For half a second, Kerko lost his footing and Jack used the Blowfish's own momentum to hurl him across the room. The alien careened into a glass cabinet, shattering it, sending the surgical instruments it contained flying everywhere. Quick as a flash, Kerko snatched up a scalpel and slashed wildly. Jack's fist connected solidly with Kerko's midriff, and the fish responded by plunging the scalpel deep into his opponent's shoulder.

Jack roared, pulling away, and Kerko scrambled up the steps towards the exit. He was bleeding profusely from the head and mouth, and although Jack wasn't in much better shape himself, he wasn't about to call a truce.

He wrenched the scalpel out of his shoulder and flung it after the Blowfish, but the blade missed and clattered harmlessly away. Seething, Jack raced after him, bounding up the steps and vaulting the rail that separated the upper Hub level from the lower. He dived for Kerko, succeeded in getting a hand to his ankle and tripped him over. Kerko sprawled and Jack was on him then.

'I have *so* had enough of you,' Jack snarled. His fingers scrabbled for the scaly throat, but Kerko batted them away, kicking and struggling all the time. Eventually Jack caught one of the flailing hands and pulled it aside, kneeling on top of the alien. Jack had the weight advantage and this was his best chance so far of finishing the fight.

But Kerko wasn't going to make it easy. 'Scum!' he roared, and then spat a mouthful of blood-stained phlegm straight into Jack's face. Jack wasn't sure if it was just a lucky shot or a Blowfish's natural defence, but the stuff *stung*. With a hiss of anger he let go and rolled away, half-blinded.

Kerko climbed to his feet, breathing hard but ready to fight again. He advanced on Jack, fists balled, inviting him to try it. They circled each other warily, treading carefully because there were live electric cables snaking across the floor, discharging sparks every now and again with sharp, burning crackles.

Kerko moved first, feinting, coming up with a left hook that Jack knocked to one side and repaid with a series of hard jabs. They exchanged blows, sometimes missing because they were too tired to aim properly now, but sometimes connecting. And when they did connect, the punches rocked. Kerko's top fin, running back over the top of his mottled head, had long since been broken and the webbed spindles flapped from side to side with every blow. Eventually, Jack managed to land a massive right cross that dislocated the fish's jaw and sent him spinning backwards. He landed face down with a huge splash in the shallow water that collected in the ditch at the base of the tower.

Jack leapt on the Blowfish and drove his knee into the back of his neck, forcing his head beneath the water. There was a sharp release of bubbles as Kerko started to gag and, teeth gritted, Jack kept his knee in position, his full weight bearing down on the fish's neck. If he could just keep his face under the water long enough…

But Kerko continued to struggle, and far from growing weaker, he seemed to be getting stronger.

And then Jack realised. Water. Fish. Good combination.

Kerko surged out of the water, twisting around and catching hold of Jack by the throat. The Blowfish's leering red face filled Jack's vision and for a moment he knew that the gleeful, homicidal light in those tiny little eyes was the last thing he would see for a while; perhaps for ever.

Kerko's fingers bit deep into Jack's throat, repeating the process he had begun so long ago in the interrogation room. His other handed curled into a fist and drove hard into Jack's gut, knocking the wind right out of him in a last, explosive *whoosh* of air. Jack's knees gave way and he sagged in the alien's grip, allowing him to turn Jack right around and hook one arm around his neck. Jack clawed weakly at the arm as it fastened around his throat and began to squeeze.

And squeeze.

Kerko was laughing now, laughing right in his ear. He could smell the guy's breath. At that moment Jack had never hated anyone so much in his life as this Blowfish. And he guessed the feeling was mutual.

He had to do something – fast.

Then his eyes found the electrical cable.

It was just out of reach, lying across the decking. The exposed wires at the end kept erupting in bright, promising sparks. There was enough voltage running through that to kill Kerko on the spot, if only Jack could use it.

He reached out with his foot, trying to hook the heel of his boot around the end and drag it towards him, into the water. It was a brilliant conductor after all. He'd seen Sean Connery do that in a film – he'd killed a guy in the bath with an electric heater. And, later on, he'd finished Oddjob in the same way – using a live cable to electrify the bars in Fort Knox.

C'mon, Jack. Stretch. You can do it. If Connery could manage it then you sure as hell can.

His heel knocked the cable once, twice. He strained every sinew in his leg and tried again, but Kerko had seen what he was doing and was dragging him back, away from the edge. Out of reach.

No good. Jack's hands let go of Kerko's arm and reached back, over his own head, trying to grab hold of the fish's head. His fingers brushed the broken spines on his skull, touched the spoon still protruding from the fleshy part. Found the webbed flaps of skin that branched out of the Blowfish's jaw line like rubbery sideburns.

And, more by luck than judgement, his fingers found their way into one of the hidden gills beneath. He felt Kerko react, clearly pained, and he dug his fingers deeper.

With a howl, Kerko let him go and Jack spun away, splashing across the pool on all fours until he could drag himself out the other side. He turned to see Kerko bearing down on him with a ferocious scream.

And then watched as the scream turned into blood-curdling shriek of pure agony.

The Blowfish straightened, stiffening, arms and fingers splayed. His head and neck went rigid and his eyes opened so wide that Jack could see the whites. His mouth gaped, the shrill scream rising in pitch as the red flesh began to bubble and blister. He began to shake violently and sparks jumped out of his mouth and anus as if he'd swallowed a firework.

Smoke poured from Kerko's gills and mouth as the flesh cooked and then, quite suddenly, it was over. The fierce, hissing crackle that had accompanied the seizure faded and all that was left was a blackened shell. It crumbled to its knees and then collapsed into the steaming water, leaving nothing but smoke and a terrible smell of fried fish.

On the far side of the pool stood Zero, one globby orange hand withdrawing from the water. Energy crackled from the thick fingertips.

'Thanks,' Jack said, 'for the shock ending.'

FIFTY-FIVE

Gwen tapped Ianto gently on the side of his face. 'Ianto!' she hissed. 'Wake up!'

His eyelids fluttered and the eye beneath rolled back into focus.

'C'mon,' Gwen insisted. 'I'm not losing you now. Not now.'

'What's the point?' he breathed. 'Look. The sky is falling.'

He gestured weakly with his hand, but Gwen didn't need to look. She had seen the boiling black clouds as they gathered ever more thickly around the gaping wound above. When she had last dared to look, the shimmering luminescence had been filled with movement, twisting and winding like a nest of glowing snakes. The edges flickered with lightning, great ragged bolts leaping to the ground beneath. Several trees and cars were in flames having already been struck, and the wind was blowing the smoke across the ruins of the Black House in dark, choking gusts.

'I know,' Gwen said. 'That's why I woke you up.'

'The sky is falling…' Ianto repeated softly. His eyes reflected the fire above.

With a loud crack, lightning forked into the ground not ten

feet away. The water in the puddles evaporated in sharp, hissing gasps and Gwen drew closer to Ianto.

'He isn't coming back,' Ianto said.

'Don't say that.'

'He'll use that wrist-strap again. That code. He'll use it to teleport himself away again.'

'Don't *say* that!'

More lightning crackled down around them, stabbing into the concrete. The rain splattered in the puddles and the wind blew harder, forcing Gwen to crouch lower. Her hair whipped around her head.

'What's happening?' she wailed.

'I told you… the sky is falling. It's getting lower. The atmospheric pressure is all shot to hell.'

The clouds were swirling, lowering still further, sweeping up leaves and twigs and lashing them angrily across the ground. More lightning smashed into the ground, sending sparks scattering around them. Glowing fragments of concrete sizzled in the puddles.

'What's that noise?' Gwen yelled over the roar of the storm.

'I can't hear anything!'

'Listen!'

They strained to hear but it was difficult over the noise of the wind and rain and lightning. But eventually, faintly, something could be heard.

A growling noise.

'Animals?' frowned Gwen.

They huddled closer, fearing the worst – dogs, or perhaps more pitbullfrogs. It was difficult to tell.

The growling increased, became a roar. Long, sustained, getting closer.

'That's not an animal,' realised Ianto.

It smashed through the railings with the deep roar of a diesel engine at full power – a single-decker bus, bouncing across the rubble and skidding to a halt in front of them. Crackling lines of energy surrounded it, jumping back and forth between the broken railings and the clouds above.

The front windscreen of the bus was shattered, obscuring the driver, but when the pneumatic doors flapped open a tall figure bounded out, greatcoat flaring behind him.

Gwen was open-mouthed in disbelief. 'Jack?'

A broad white grin spilt Jack's face. 'Hi, kids!' he laughed. 'Miss me?'

'Where the hell have you been?'

'I had to fetch someone,' he said. 'You may know him.'

Something moved in the bus, something glowing with a fierce orange light. As it moved, electricity crackled around the bus in fierce, jagged sparks. It followed Jack off the bus, stepping down amid a web of fizzing energy.

'Zero,' said Ianto.

As the orange jelly creature walked slowly towards them, the effect on the sky above was instant and profound.

The clouds suddenly seemed to part and the oily light above bulged downwards in a vast, inverted dome shape. It looked like a gigantic bubble, full of swirling colours. Lightning flowed from the clouds down to the earth, leaping across the concrete in flashing sparks until it reached Zero. Then the energy rose up him, flowing over him, caressing him.

'What's happening?' Gwen cried over the crackling discharges.

'Reunion!' Jack yelled back. The rain swirled in the wind, plastering his black hair against his forehead as he watched Zero absorb the lightning bolts.

'What do you mean?'

'I said Zero was lost,' Jack told them, his eyes never leaving the alien. 'Lost and alone – trapped here on Earth. Well…' He pointed up into the sky as the swelling bubble of colours. 'That's Mom. She's come looking for her boy.'

Gwen stared, wide eyed. 'But – what is it? Where's it from?'

'It's a Vortex Dweller,' said Jack. 'No one knows what they're really called, or anything much about them – apart from the fact that they exist in the Time Vortex. It's extremely rare to even glimpse such a thing. But occasionally, once in a million years, they break through into our universe.'

Zero's bright orange colour suddenly turned a deeper, darker shade and then red, scarlet, purple, blue and green. The colours flowed through him like oil in water, and he instantly resembled the vast creature above.

'The lightning is how they communicate here,' Jack was grinning again. 'Electricity for words – get that!'

'You mean every time Zero electrocuted someone he was just saying hello?'

'Yeah!' Jack was laughing, although he suddenly became serious. 'I mean, yeah, something like that… It's kinda tragic – but it was an honest mistake. He never meant anyone harm. He just wanted to go home.'

Zero was floating high into the air as they spoke, borne aloft by flickering tendrils of energy. He was heading up towards the creature in the clouds, pulled towards it in a fierce, crackling embrace.

Gwen was on her feet, and she was smiling at the sight. 'But why – how come the mother has only come now?'

'My guess? She's been looking for him – and the temporal fusion bomb has blown open a hole in time and space big enough for her to peep through.'

Zero flew up and up, surrounded by lightning, and suddenly merged into the coruscating colours above.

'Mommy's come for him,' Jack cried. 'She must have been worried sick and now she's got her baby back again.' He grabbed Gwen and Ianto and kissed them both. 'Oh boy, do I love a happy ending!'

'Happy ending?' repeated Ianto. 'Are you serious? Cardiff has been *totally destroyed*!'

'It ain't over yet.' Jack squeezed Ianto close, still smiling. 'What would any worried parent do when they found their lost child?'

'Well, I don't know, I'm not a parent. But I imagine they'd be pretty relieved.'

'They'd be very grateful,' realised Gwen.

Jack laughed again. 'You said it.'

And with that, he patted them both on the backside and walked forward alone, looking up at the flickering light show. Zero was now nowhere to be seen, but the shimmering bulge of the parent was still sending bolts of lightning down to earth.

Jack stopped beneath it, still looking straight up, and raised his arms.

'No,' said Gwen. 'Oh no…'

And the lightning suddenly converged on Jack, picking him up like a leaf in the wind, scouring through skin and bone, illuminating him from within.

And his screams were awful to hear.

LAST ORDERS

FIFTY-SIX

It was quiet in the pub. It had been quiet all week. The landlord was beginning to wonder if anything was ever going to happen. Cardiff was a wonderful city but sometimes the paying customers needed a bit of a kick up the arse. What he needed was another International at the Millennium Stadium, or another Olympic homecoming, to help bring the punters in.

He sighed, wiping dry the last pint glass. It was nearly throwing-out time and there were only one or two tables with anyone still sitting down. He decided to give it another five minutes before he rang the bell. The three people at the far table looked like they were having a serious conversation, and he was in a generous mood, even if they hadn't been drinking much.

The two students were nursing their drinks – half a bitter for the lad and a rum and coke for the girl.

The older bloke, clean-cut type in a grey military overcoat, had a glass of water. The landlord remembered him getting the round in. He was a yank, and they were always a bit odd. Good tippers, though.

Jack Harkness pushed the two little white dots across the table.

His two companions regarded them dubiously.

'It's your choice,' Jack said quietly.

Rachel Banks looked up at him, straight into his eyes. She could always tell when someone was lying to her. But all she saw in those blue eyes was truth and sincerity. She turned to Wynnie. 'What do you think?'

He held her hand tightly. 'Voluntary amnesia? I dunno… my mind's in a bit of a muddle as it is, to be honest.'

'These pills will un-muddle things for you,' said Jack. 'It will be like the last couple of days never happened. You'll go home, go to bed, and wake up not remembering a thing about it. Hell, you're students – you must be used to that.'

'I don't know,' Ray said. She looked back at the little white pills. 'I don't do drugs. Not ever.'

'Me neither,' said Wynnie. He looked at Jack, then shrugged. 'Well, not much. I mean, nothing serious. But these…'

'Let me just recap,' Jack said patiently. 'You have both been through a terrible ordeal. Seeing the funeral cortège, tracking down the pallbearers to the Black House. Meeting Gwen and going down into the cellars… all of that happened. There was more—'

'I know,' Ray said quietly, flinching. 'I thought things were bad before – but that… those creatures, the gunfire…' She looked at Wynnie and squeezed his hand in both of hers, leaving the sentence unfinished.

'It got worse than that, believe me,' Jack said. 'Unimaginably worse.'

'How?'

'I can't explain that now, and I won't even try. Because it doesn't matter. But things were put right again – changed, completely and in ways you can't imagine or understand. But it will have affected you in ways you may not like, and if you tell anyone about it they won't ever believe you. That goes for me, Gwen, Torchwood – the whole lot. You can't write about it, you can't blog it, you can't go to the newspapers. That can be a hard thing to bear.'

'We have each other,' Wynnie pointed out.

'That's why I'm giving you the option.'

'And what about Gillian?' Ray asked. 'She saw it all too.'

'She's probably already sold her story to *Hello*,' said Wynnie.

'My colleagues are meeting with Gillian,' Jack said.

Jack's tone, coupled with a twitch of a smile, suggested that there was more to it than just a meeting, and Wynnie raised an eyebrow. 'You're gonna make Gillian forget everything, aren't you? You're not giving her the choice.'

'That's horrible,' Ray whispered.

'It's sensible,' argued Wynnie. 'You know Gillian can't hold her own water at the best of times. And with all this in her head... She'd blab to anyone who'd listen.'

'Yes, but—'

'And she'd be made into a laughing stock,' Wynnie continued thoughtfully, as the implications mounted up. 'Everyone would think she was mad. I mean, we know she *is*, but not like that.'

Ray just stared at the tablets on the table and said nothing.

'*That* would be horrible,' Wynnie told her softly. 'She doesn't deserve that, does she? Better she comes back as the old Gillian, with nothing in her head at all.'

Even Ray had to smile at that, just a little. 'Maybe. But why are we being treated differently?'

'I wanted to see you two together,' said Jack simply. They both frowned back at him, puzzled, not quite understanding. But they would. They still hadn't stopped holding hands. Jack smiled at them and then finished the last of his water. He stood up. 'It's your choice,' he said. 'You call it.'

Later, by the waterfront at Mermaid Quay, he caught up with Gwen and Ianto.

They were battered and bruised – Gwen's ankle was strapped

up and she was using a walking stick, temporarily, and there were some minor cuts and contusions on her face that Jack had assured her would be healed by the time Rhys returned home.

Ianto was in a worse state, of course, although it hardly showed. He was wearing a rather smart Burberry overcoat over a new suit, which hid the heavy bandages Jack knew were wrapped around his chest. A lot of the damage had been undone, but there were still sores. There would probably be scars.

But he did look good in that coat.

Jack, of course, looked as fresh as ever – there would never be any physical scars for him. What hurt him remained inside.

Gwen smiled at him as he walked up, pulling a strand of hair from her face that was being blown by the wind as it came in across the bay in cold, damp gusts. 'How did it go?'

'Pretty good,' Jack said. He thrust his hands into his greatcoat pockets and looked out across the shimmering water. The sky was overcast and there was the promise of rain. There always was. And there always would be.

'Did they take the Retcon?' Ianto asked.

'I left it to them.'

'What?'

Jack smiled knowingly. 'It's their call. Ray and Wynnie found something awful, it's true – something that some might consider best forgotten. But they found something else, too – something in each other that's too good and rare to lose. It's their decision.'

Ianto looked at Gwen and pulled a face.

Jack laughed. 'You know I'm just a big softie really.'

'So,' Gwen said, 'let's see if I've got this straight: the Vortex Dweller put everything right in gratitude for us returning its baby. It rewound time or something to a point before the temporal fusion device went off?'

'You were closer with your first guess,' Jack said. 'It didn't actually alter time – no big button to reset everything. It just… put everything back in its right place. Think of it like a great big jigsaw puzzle. It was all broken up, but now every piece is back in its proper place. The picture is complete. And it's a good one – with no pallbearers, no fusion device, none of the extra stuff that was coming through the Rift because of the Hokrala Corp. No Kerko – and I sure won't miss him. There are cracks, of course – and people have a hazy memory of something happening. A minor earthquake during the night. It can happen, even in Cardiff.'

'But the Vortex Dweller brought Ray and Wynnie and Gillian back to life.'

'You can think of it like that, yeah.'

'But what about Frank Morgan?'

'He stays dead. There's nothing for him here now. And he was dead by 1915.'

'It's incredible,' Gwen said, 'that all those things and events could be just... edited out... and yet everything else remains untouched. It doesn't seem possible.'

'Gives me a headache just thinking about it,' said Ianto.

Jack smiled. 'The Vortex Dwellers are pan-dimensional beings, way above us in any terms you care to think of. Repairing everything and everybody that had been damaged by the Undertaker's Gift was easy – like us mopping up milk spilled by a child. We can't even conceive of the complexities involved – but the Vortex Dwellers can. They can do stuff like that to our universe in the blink of an eye.'

Ianto blew out his cheeks, impressed. 'Good job they stay where they are, then.'

'Isn't it?' Jack agreed.

'But in order for them to do that, to understand what was needed, you had to communicate with them,' Gwen said. She linked Jack's arm and pulled him close. 'And they use lightning for words, you said. You were electrocuted over and over again.'

'I had a lot to ask,' Jack admitted.

'It must have hurt.'

'Not as much as seeing this place destroyed,' Jack replied. His face grew serious at the memory. 'I never wanna see that again. Ever.'

He let his gaze wander back to the Bay area, the shops and the city beyond. There was no sign of the destruction that had been wreaked now. All was calm. Every building and road was intact, no smoke, no storm clouds. The three of them stood in silence for a short while, in memory of a hellish vision of the world that had come so close to being real. And they would remember it for the rest of their lives – for them, Retcon was never an option.

'There is one other thing,' Jack said eventually. 'The Vortex Dweller knew all about the Rift. It could see it running right through Cardiff, right through Earth, clear as day. It asked if I wanted it repaired – closed up for ever.'

Gwen and Ianto looked at him, shocked. 'What, honestly?' Gwen asked. 'It actually *offered* to seal the Rift?'

'It could do that?' wondered Ianto.

'Oh yeah,' Jack nodded. 'Easy as pie. A stitch in time – done in a second. Those Vortex Dwellers, I'm telling ya, they don't mess around. And with the Rift gone, there would be no more time distortion in Cardiff, no more flotsam and jetsam coming through from all points in time and space for us to clear up. Job done, over, *finito*.'

Gwen and Ianto could hardly take it in. 'But that would mean—' Gwen began.

'No more Torchwood,' said Ianto. 'Our job here would be over.'

'Guess so,' Jack nodded.

There was a short silence.

'So… what did you say?' Gwen asked.

'I said no,' Jack replied easily.

'No?'

'That's right.' Jack heaved a sigh. 'Well, I thought it was asking a bit much after all the repair work, and anyway, you two would be out of a job and I'd just end up bored out of my mind… it seemed simpler in the end to leave it as it was.'

He put his arms around them and hugged them close. Ianto winced a little.

'I did ask for a tiny little tweak to be made, though,' Jack continued. 'The Rift runs through time as well as space, obviously, so I got the Vortex Dweller to just pinch it shut at a particular point in the future. The forty-ninth century to be exact.'

'Isn't that when the Hokrala Corp come from?' asked Ianto.

'Let's just say we won't be getting any more visits from them.'

'That is good news.'

'Hey,' Jack was smiling again, lifting his face towards the sky. 'With us here, it's *always* good news.'

Acknowledgements

I am extremely grateful for being given the opportunity to write another *Torchwood* story. My thanks to Steve Tribe, patient and considerate editor, and to Gary Russell and all at BBC Wales. I hope I've done you all proud.

There are many other people in the production team who deserve a mention – too many to thank individually, but I can't let the chance go by without offering heartfelt praise and congratulations to all the producers and in particular the people who make writing about Jack, Gwen and Ianto so easy – so here's to you, John, Eve and Gareth. And a special thank you to Russell T Davies, for creating such lovely characters in the first place – and letting me include one or two guest cameos in this book!

There is a host of people at BBC Books to thank, too – not least of which are Lee Binding, the cover artist, Kari Speers for proofreading, and the Big Chief himself, Albert DePetrillo.

Special mention, as ever, to my good friend Pete Stam. And a special 'shout out' for Phil Macklin and Matty Ellison!

And last but not least, I am grateful to my family – Martine, Luke and Konnie, to whom I dedicate all my books because I simply wouldn't be able to write them without their support and patience. This one meant a lot of very late nights (again) and, more often than not, a thoughtful, frowning silence as I thought about plot problems when I should have been doing something else entirely. I'm very lucky having all of you.

TORCHWOOD
ALMOST PERFECT
James Goss

ISBN 978 1 846 07573 5
£6.99

Emma is 30, single and frankly desperate. She woke up this morning with nothing to look forward to but another evening of unsuccessful speed-dating. But now she has a new weapon in her quest for Mr Right. And it's made her almost perfect.

Gwen Cooper woke up this morning expecting the unexpected. As usual. She went to work and found a skeleton at a table for two and a colleague in a surprisingly glamorous dress. Perfect.

Ianto Jones woke up this morning with no memory of last night. He went to work, where he caused amusement, suspicion and a little bit of jealousy. Because Ianto Jones woke up this morning in the body of a woman. And he's looking just about perfect.

Jack Harkness has always had his doubts about Perfection.

Featuring Captain Jack Harkness as played by John Barrowman, with Gwen Cooper and Ianto Jones as played by Eve Myles and Gareth David-Lloyd, in the hit series created by Russell T Davies for BBC Television.

T O R C H W O O D
INTO THE SILENCE
Sarah Pinborough

ISBN 978 1 846 07753 1
£6.99

The body in the church hall is very definitely dead. It has been sliced open with surgical precision, its organs exposed, and its vocal cords are gone. It is as if they were never there or they've been dissolved…

With the Welsh Amateur Operatic Contest getting under way, music is filling the churches and concert halls of Cardiff. The competition has attracted the finest Welsh talent to the city, but it has also drawn something else – there are stories of a metallic creature hiding in the shadows. Torchwood are on its tail, but it's moving too fast for them to track it down.

This new threat requires a new tactic – so Ianto Jones is joining a male voice choir…

Featuring Captain Jack Harkness as played by John Barrowman, with Gwen Cooper and Ianto Jones as played by Eve Myles and Gareth David-Lloyd, in the hit series created by Russell T Davies for BBC Television.

T O R C H W O O D
BAY OF THE DEAD
Mark Morris

ISBN 978 1 846 07737 1
£6.99

When the city sleeps, the dead start to walk…

Something has sealed off Cardiff, and living corpses are stalking the streets, leaving a trail of half-eaten bodies. Animals are butchered. A young couple in their car never reach their home. A stolen yacht is brought back to shore, carrying only human remains. And a couple of girls heading back from the pub watch the mysterious drivers of a big black SUV take over a crime scene.

Torchwood have to deal with the intangible barrier surrounding Cardiff, and some unidentified space debris that seems to be regenerating itself. Plus, of course, the all-night zombie horror show.

Not that they really believe in zombies.

Featuring Captain Jack Harkness as played by John Barrowman, with Gwen Cooper and Ianto Jones as played by Eve Myles and Gareth David-Lloyd, in the hit series created by Russell T Davies for BBC Television.

Jackson Leaves – an Edwardian house in Penylan, built 1906, semi-detached, three storeys, spacious, beautifully presented. Left in good condition to Rob and Julia by Rob's late aunt.

It's an ordinary sort of a house. Except for the way the rooms don't stay in the same places. And the strange man that turns up in the airing cupboard. And the apparitions. And the temporal surges that attract the attentions of Torchwood.

And the fact that the first owner of Jackson Leaves in 1906 was a Captain Jack Harkness...

Featuring Captain Jack Harkness as played by John Barrowman, with Gwen Cooper and Ianto Jones as played by Eve Myles and Gareth David-Lloyd, in the hit series created by Russell T Davies for BBC Television.

Also available from BBC Books

T O R C H W O O D
RISK ASSESSMENT
James Goss

ISBN 978 1 846 07783 8
£6.99

'Are you trying to tell me, Captain Harkness, that the entire staff of Torchwood Cardiff now consists of yourself, a woman in trousers and a tea boy?'

Agnes Haversham is awake, and Jack is worried (and not a little afraid). The Torchwood Assessor is roused from her deep sleep in only the worst of times – it's happened just four times in the last 100 years. Can the situation really be so bad?

Someone, somewhere, is fighting a war, and they're losing badly. The coffins of the dead are coming through the Rift. With thousands of alien bodies floating in the Bristol Channel, it's down to Torchwood to round them all up before a lethal plague breaks out.

And now they'll have to do it by the book. The 1901 edition.

Featuring Captain Jack Harkness as played by John Barrowman, with Gwen Cooper and Ianto Jones as played by Eve Myles and Gareth David-Lloyd, in the hit series created by Russell T Davies for BBC Television.

T O R C H W O O D
THE UNDERTAKER'S GIFT
Trevor Baxendale

ISBN 978 1 846 07782 1
£6.99

The Hokrala Corp lawyers are back. They're suing planet Earth for mishandling the twenty-first century, and they won't tolerate any efforts to repel them. An assassin has been sent to remove Captain Jack Harkness.

It's been a busy week in Cardiff. The Hub's latest guest is a translucent, amber jelly carrying a lethal electrical charge. Record numbers of aliens have been coming through the Rift, and Torchwood could do without any more problems.

But there are reports of an extraordinary funeral cortège in the night-time city, with mysterious pallbearers guarding a rotting cadaver that simply doesn't want to be buried.

Torchwood should be ready for anything – but with Jack the target of an invisible killer, Gwen trapped in a forgotten crypt and Ianto Jones falling desperately ill, could a world of suffering be the Undertaker's gift to planet Earth?

Featuring Captain Jack Harkness as played by John Barrowman, with Gwen Cooper and Ianto Jones as played by Eve Myles and Gareth David-Lloyd, in the hit series created by Russell T Davies for BBC Television.

THE
TORCHWOOD
ARCHIVES

ISBN 978 1 846 07459 2

£14.99

Separate from the Government
Outside the police
Beyond the United Nations…

Founded by Queen Victoria in 1879, the Torchwood Institute has long battled against alien threats to the British Empire. The Torchwood Archives is an insider's look into the secret world of this unique investigative team.

In-depth background on personnel, case files on alien enemies of the Crown and descriptions of extra-terrestrial technology collected over the years will uncover more about the world of Torchwood than ever previously known, including some of the biggest mysteries surrounding the Rift in space and time running through Cardiff.

Based on the hit series created by Russell T Davies for BBC Television.

TORCHWOOD
THE ENCYCLOPEDIA
Gary Russell

ISBN 978 1 846 07764 7
£14.99

Founded by Queen Victoria in 1879, the Torchwood Institute has been defending Great Britain from the alien hordes for 130 years. Though London's Torchwood One was destroyed during the Battle of Canary Wharf, the small team at Torchwood Three have continued to monitor the space-time Rift that runs through Cardiff, saving the world and battling for the future of the human race.

Now you can discover every fact and figure, explore every crack in time and encounter every creature that Torchwood have dealt with. Included here are details of:

- The secret of the Children of Earth

- Operatives from Alice Guppy to Gwen Cooper

- Extraterrestrial visitors from Arcateenians to Weevils

- The life and deaths of Captain Jack Harkness

and much more. Illustrated throughout with photos and artwork from all three series, this A–Z provides everything you need to know about Torchwood.

Based on the hit series created by Russell T Davies for BBC Television.